THEY LOVE ME KNOT

RAELYNN ROSE

❀ Created with Vellum

TRIGGER WARNINGS:

Before you start Sophie's story, I think I should offer a few warnings. While this book does contain a happily ever after, it is intended for mature audiences only. As an alternate universe story, there are mentions of knots, heats, breeding, and lots of detailed and spicy sex scenes that may contain more than two participants. If that's not for you, turn back now.

Graphic sex, violence, cursing, and dominant alphas abound in this book. There is mild sexual manipulation as well as some physical abuse (not by the MC). I tried to do my best to broach varying subjects with sensitivity, but please take care of yourself and stop reading if anything triggers a sense of anxiety or fear.

Wait! Have you joined the party yet? Oops...I meant the newsletter! Keep up to date on releases, cover reveals, and giveaways, as well as a free novella. You can join here!

CHAPTER 1

Sophie

L ugging one of my suitcases up the stairs, I glared at the alpha who stood at the doorway, holding it open, watching me struggle.

"No. It's fine. I've got it," I mumbled under my breath as I passed.

The door closed behind me and I turned to find him staring. After a few minutes, my mouth refused to stay shut.

"Are you going to show me to my room, or am I supposed to guess?"

A sound similar to a growl rumbled from his broad chest, but he jerked his head for me to follow him down the hall and pushed the second door on the right open. Reaching around the wall, he flipped on the light, then left me standing there.

Malakai – Kai – Janse was the alpha responsible for watching over me while my parents sought a pack to court me in hopes of finally seeing their twenty-eight-year-old spinster omega daughter shacked up.

I was the youngest of three omega siblings and the last to find a pack. Not for a lack of trying. I'd met with alphas. I had met with packs. I didn't even care whether the packs had a beta in the mix.

What I cared about was the fact each pack expected me to turn my back on pursuing a life outside of breeding and carrying pups, of increasing the population of alphas or omegas. As if I had a choice in what designation my body would create.

It didn't matter what I wanted. My genes dictated my future with or without my permission.

Hoisting the suitcase onto the bed, I turned and studied my surroundings. It was a decent sized room with a bed big enough to share if I actually found anyone with whom I would want to actually share it.

An ensuite bathroom was on a far wall, a walk-in closet open and ready for me to hang my clothes. I had no idea how long I would be here, how long it would take my parents to rifle through the stack of applications they'd received when I'd finally relented and told them I was ready for a pack.

I wasn't. I wasn't ready to give my life over completely to another person. I had planned to put my master's in omega social work to use, to help others navigate the world that saw them as inferior.

Tears burned the backs of my eyes. Stress strung my nerves taut, and I wanted to scream, to throw something against the wall simply for the satisfaction of watching it shatter.

Heavy footsteps thudded down the hall. Blinking rapidly, I squared my shoulders, lifted my chin, and popped open my suitcase so I could start putting my clothing in drawers or hang them in the closet before everything wrinkled.

Kai stepped in carrying the last two suitcases and set them on the floor beside the bed, bowing at the waist with a forced smile. "There you go, princess," he said in a deep voice before turning on his heel and leaving the room.

Princess? Did he seriously just call me princess?

I supposed it would be accurate if he was referring to the kind that was locked in a tower while waiting for some magnanimous prince to rescue me.

Because that was my current situation – I was to reside in this form of a halfway house while my parents found a pack suitable for their omega daughter, someone who could help them continue their rise up the social ladder.

I was a pawn. No different than my sister and brother. My parents would find a pack full of big, strong alphas with important roles in government or maybe finance. As long as they could whisk me off to some palace, to shower me with gifts and trinkets and then fill my belly with pups.

Princess. Fine. He wanted a princess, he would get one.

He'd been hired by my parents. From the little they'd told me, he was a member of Omega Rescue and Extraction. No idea why he was on omega babysitting duty, but no way would I be allowed to live alone, not unbonded and unclaimed.

I might have slammed the drawers closed a little too hard each time I'd filled them, but it was the closest I could get to breaking stuff. And at the moment, there wasn't much else I could do to expel the angry energy that was starting to burn through my veins, quickly pushing away the fear and anxiety over my future.

Looking around the room, I wasn't exactly repulsed. It was a pretty enough room, albeit plain. But it wasn't my room. And I didn't see a nest.

My parents probably had high hopes I would find a pack before my next cycle hit so I could go right into breeding.

If only they knew how long I'd been on birth control. I'd dabbled with suppressants, but there were no full studies on the effects of long-term suppressant use and I did want to become a mother some-day. No reason to tempt fate and render myself sterile with experimental drugs.

Tucking the empty suitcases into the back of the closet, I straightened my clothes, smoothed my hands over my hair, then stepped from the room in search of my babysitter.

Kai was sprawled on the couch, the remote in his hand and pointed at the TV.

"Are you going to give me a tour of the place?"

His brows drew up and together in confusion. "You saw your bedroom. This is the living room. The kitchen is over there," he said, pointing over his shoulder at the kitchen visible in the open concept house.

"Okay. Nest?" I said, my blonde brows drawing together at his absolute lack of respect or give a shit.

It took him a second of staring at me, his nostrils flaring, before he pushed to a sitting position, throwing his legs over the side of the couch. "You're not in heat."

"No shit. You must be psychic."

His lips twitched at the corners, and I had the urge to cross the room and smack the smirk off his face.

He was handsome. There was no denying it. He had striking sky blue eyes, inky black hair, a patrician nose, and a neat beard that drew my attention to his lips.

All things I had no desire to notice, damn it.

With a grunt, he pushed to his feet and stalked toward me. The closer he got, the more I had to crane my neck to look into his face. Surely, this alpha didn't think he could intimidate me.

Not only did I have to crane my neck, but I had to hold my breath as he got within touching distance of me. The man smelled like sex. Well, not sex exactly, but his heady woodsy scent was mixed with something that reminded me of fresh baked cookies – vanilla and brown sugar and so much yumminess.

And that stupid smirk was back on his face as he stared down at me for a second, then passed me, heading for the hall.

My panties were damp as slick coated my core from his scent and his proximity. No way would I allow this neanderthal to cause me to lose myself simply because he smelled edible.

"In here," he grumbled.

Rolling my head on my shoulders and wincing at the crack of my neck, I turned and followed where he stepped into the first door on the left. The door was opened to a room full of pillows and blankets and a bed that could fit ten people easily. It looked soft and smelled heavily of cleaning products and scent canceling detergents.

"Thank you. That wasn't so hard, was it?" I said, shooting him my own smirk before tossing my hair over my shoulder and trying my hardest not to stomp away with Kai still at my back.

He'd barely said more than five words to me. He'd called me a princess. He resorted to animalistic grunting rather than articulating a thought. And he crowded my space.

My parents needed to get through the stack of applicants quickly. Because if I had to stay here with Kai any longer than necessary, I had a feeling I would end up smacking the smug look off his face.

Kai

I WAS A TRAINED FUCKING SOLDIER. I had done several tours in the military. Countless rescue missions with my team of ORE. Until I had lost two of those teammates.

Now? I was on babysitting duty until further notice.

The two of us remaining members of my team had been displaced until our commander was either able to find new recruits to rebuild a full team, or until we could be absorbed into an existing and active team.

Suburban life wasn't exactly something I strived for. It wasn't something I wanted. In fact, it was something I had avoided my entire adult life.

Here I was, smack in the middle of a neighborhood, surrounded by identical houses with identical situations housing spoiled omegas waiting for their prince – more like princes – to whisk them away to their palace where they could live the life of their dreams. They could sit around being doted on, go shopping, decorate their mansions, and drag their alphas into the nest for big ol' orgies every cycle.

Not that the last part was a bad thing. But it was the type of domesticity I didn't want.

I wanted to go back to fucking work. I wanted to eliminate more compounds like the one we'd invaded while attempting to rescue as many omegas as possible.

At least I was getting paid to sit around with my thumb up my ass while the princess shopped for her future pack.

My primary job was escorting the unbonded omega if she needed to leave the house, keeping overzealous alphas from sniffing around, and keeping her safe when packs came to meet her in hopes of getting her permission to court her.

Me. I, alone, was supposed to watch over her when packs of alphas showed up to get to know her, to woo her.

Not that I was scared. Even outnumbered, I highly doubted the alphas had even a quarter of the training I'd received through the years. Nor the stash of weapons.

After Sophie checked out the nest, she stood in the middle of the living room and looked around as I took my position back on the couch. It was exactly where I planned to spend a majority of my time while on this particular mission. And that was how I needed to think of it, otherwise I would go fucking nuts.

From the corner of my eye, I watched as she crossed her arms over her chest and turned in a slow circle. There wasn't much to look at; the place was nice and spacious, but the only walls were around the bathrooms and bedrooms.

And there was a basement, but I couldn't picture the dainty princess daring to venture into the dungeon to lift weights. She might muss her hair or break a nail.

Turning my head, I let my eyes roam her from head to toe before she caught me staring. No doubt I'd get an ass chewing for daring to look at her.

She was pretty. Okay, she was more than pretty. Her blonde hair hung in perfect waves nearly to her waist. She was petite, had a tiny waist, round hips, a tight little ass, and perky tits. Her lips were a little on the thinner side. That, added with the smatter of freckles, gave her an air of girl next door, or like she'd grown up on a farm instead of whatever mansion she'd been raised in.

Her clothes looked expensive but fuck if I had a clue who the shit was made by. I liked my jeans and tees when I wasn't donned in my black fatigues for work.

But yeah…she was hot. And she smelled good, even beneath whatever she'd used to hide her scent. It was something sweet and floral, like lilacs in the spring and something else, something sugary like caramel.

Her feet were encased in a pair of heels. Fucking heels. Like she was going on a date instead of moving into a halfway house for unbonded omegas.

"Do you mind?" she snapped at me, dragging my attention back to her face.

Well, shit. I hadn't been fast enough and she'd caught me staring.

Rolling my shoulders, I refocused on the TV and shrugged. "Trying to figure out why the fuck you're wearing those things inside the house."

I could see her bend and look at her feet from my periphery, and I had to hide the smile when she stepped out of them and carried them back to her room.

A few minutes later, she exited wearing a pair of worn jeans – not the kind that had seen a lot of physical labor, but like the kind she bought fashionably distressed – and a sweater.

"There. Better?" she asked, holding her arms out to her side and doing a dramatic twirl.

"I don't care what you wear. I'm not the one courting you."

She huffed an exasperated sound, then finally crossed the living room and flopped onto one of the recliners. And then she was back to crossing her arms over her chest, her legs crossed at the knees instead of kicking the recliner back and relaxing.

"It could be days before your first visitors. Might as well get comfortable," I said without looking at her.

"That's what I'm worried about," she muttered.

Glancing at her over my shoulder, I frowned. "You're a pretty omega. I'm sure someone will be willing to put up with you."

Sophie gaped at me, her mouth literally hanging open as her scent turned a little bitter with her indignant anger.

"Excuse me? Put up with *me*?" Her legs uncrossed and she sat up straight. "What the hell is your problem? What did I do to you to deserve to be treated like I'm some kind of inconvenience?"

I whirled my legs over the couch and sat up, prepared to launch into a speech about how I was supposed to be saving lives, not pampering a spoiled ass omega. But when I spotted the glimmering in her pretty brown eyes, the insults and retort were frozen in my throat.

Fuck. Fucking hell. I didn't want to be here, and she was obviously used to a different type of lifestyle than the one she'd have while here, but she didn't deserve to have an asshole like me taking my personal issues out on her.

With a growl, I pushed to my feet and stormed from the room, crossing through the kitchen and heading for the basement door. A sniffle stalled my feet and the urge to rush back into the room and console her was nearly overwhelming.

I didn't calm omegas. I didn't hold them and comfort them. I saved them from shitty situations and helped them find somewhere safe if they didn't have a family to return to.

Clenching my jaw, I continued to the basement door, yanking it open too hard, and nearly sprinted down the stairs into the dark area. The space wasn't finished, concrete walls and concrete floor making the lower level cold and emotionless.

But it had a weight bench and a punching bag. I had to get this energy out, had to pound my fists against the heavy bag until all I felt was the sting of my knuckles instead of the regret I suddenly felt over making Sophie feel like shit.

None of this was her fault. Her designation wasn't her fault. The fact her family would rather pawn her off on a pack of strangers rather than allow her to remain an unbonded omega wasn't her fault.

Yet, I'd just reminded her that she was low man on the totem pole, reminded her of how few choices she had in her life.

I was a fucking asshole.

CHAPTER 2

Sophie

Kai leaned against the wall near the kitchen and watched my interaction with the four alphas sitting around the room. They were pleasant enough, but something was…missing.

I couldn't put my finger on it. The fact one of them smelled like burned popcorn wasn't exactly appealing. And the alpha on the far left of the couch couldn't seem to keep his eyes on my face and instead constantly ran them over my body as though he was trying to see through the dress I'd chosen for my very first meeting arranged by my parents.

No matter how hard I tried, I couldn't stop visually checking in with Kai. His eyes were watchful, and it was obvious he wasn't a fan of any of the men firing questions at me left and right, even if he looked the epitome of cool, calm, and collected.

"When was your last heat?" one of the guys asked. I could barely remember their names. His started with a J…Jake? James? Jason?

That alone was a bad sign, the fact I couldn't remember their names and was a little turned off by their scents.

Now, throw in the fact this guy was asking something super personal, I was more than ready for this meeting to be over.

"Excuse me?"

"We want to make sure you're regular. Our goal is a family. An infertile omega isn't acceptable."

A soft growl trickled from where Kai stood. He made a show of checking the time and pushed from the wall. "I'm sorry, gentleman, but Miss Cannon has another appointment to attend. It's time to say goodnight."

"She has another meeting this late? With who? Another pack?" another of the guys asked. I didn't even remember what letter his name started with, let alone his actual name.

His nostrils flared as though he was scenting the air.

"How many packs do you plan to court at once?"

Tilting my head to the side, I blinked at him. Then blinked again. "I hadn't really made up my mind, actually. What do you think, Kai?" I looked at him over my shoulder. "Three? Five? I mean, why limit my options?" I said, turning my attention back to the asshole now glaring at me.

"This is a waste of time. I have no intention of bonding with someone who's spreading her legs for anyone and everyone she meets."

He pushed to his feet the same time Kai pushed from the wall. With a flick of my hand, I motioned Kai to stay where he was and watched the men leave with a forced smile on my lips.

"I'm not sure how you think you're some kind of prize with that attitude. You're pushing thirty, your personality is lacking, and your tits don't match your confidence."

"Time to go," Kai said, this time not bothering to check in with me.

He marched forward, snatching the asshole by the collar and nearly dragging him to the door. His three packmates looked as though they would charge Kai's back, try to sucker punch him when his back was turned, but Kai was faster and stronger than all three.

With the door pushed open, he began shoving until all four alphas were through the door and on the porch.

A cool breeze ruffled my hair as Kai slammed the door shut and turned the locks into place.

"Fucking assholes," he muttered under his breath. "Told the commander I didn't want to deal with this shit." He continued mumbling under his breath as he'd done the first day I'd arrived, and stomped across the room and into the basement where a barrage of booms and thuds sounded through the floor accompanied by a rattle of chain and creaking of the floorboards.

It had only been a few days, but I'd learned his tells. He always stomped downstairs when he didn't know what to say, when something pissed him off or stressed him out.

Unfortunately, that something was usually me. It was obvious he hated being here and wasn't overly fond of me.

But I was thankful for his presence tonight.

Hurrying to my bedroom, I changed from the dress into a pair of sleep pants and a t-shirt, then twisted my curled hair into a low bun. I'd wash my makeup off before bed. For now, I wanted him to know that whether either of us liked our current situation, I appreciated what he'd done for me tonight, that he was willing to watch over me and keep assholes like those who'd just been tossed out of the house from making me uncomfortable. Or worse.

I kept my feet bare as I hurried through the house and followed the sounds into the basement I had yet to explore. What was there for me to do down there? I didn't lift weights. I'd never thrown a punch in my life. And Kai had said it wasn't finished, simply a storage space.

And honestly…basements creeped me out a little.

The stairs creaked under each of my steps, but the pounding didn't cease.

There was only dim lighting from a few fluorescent lights hanging from the drop ceiling overhead. But it was enough.

Kai had pulled his shirt off and was squared up to the bag as though it was an opponent and repeatedly punched it, causing the rattle of the chains I heard through the floor. His arms hadn't given anything away when he'd worn t-shirts, but most of his torso was covered in a tapestry of ink, the designs unique yet flowing to create the most beautiful landscape along his muscular body.

When he swung his left first, he twisted enough for me to catch a jagged scar along his left shoulder, reaching from his neck to the bottom of his shoulder blade. The skin was silvery pink and puckered as though it wasn't that old. Or had been one hell of an injury.

The next swing was with his right hand, and he caught sight of me from the corner of his eye and froze.

I was at least twenty feet away, but even from here, I could smell his warm, sweet scent carrying to me. Everything south of my belly-button throbbed and begged for attention, and my head began to swim with want. With need.

Kai's broad, shimmering chest heaved as he gulped in deep breaths, his eyes steady on mine, the icy blueness freezing me in my spot.

"You good?" he asked, his deep voice feeling as though it touched places deep inside of me.

"I, uh...thank you," I blurted when I realized I was still staring at him and worried I'd begun to drool.

His raven dark brows puckered. "For what?"

Jerking my head toward the stairs, I said, "For kicking those guys out. And for...well, for being here. In case other packs are like that. I know you don't want to be here. I don't either. I wanted..."

Kai turned to face me full on, his hands on his hips. "You wanted what?" he asked after a few seconds.

"I had plans for my life. And being at the sexual beck and call of a pack of alphas wasn't on that list."

"Then why are you here?"

My brows shot up my forehead. "I don't have a choice. You know that."

His head nodded up and down a few times, but he didn't say anything. His nostrils flared then he took a deliberate step back.

Did he not like my scent? Because I sure as hell wanted to bathe in his. I wanted to have that taste on my tongue until I was suffering a sugar high and maybe even a few cavities.

After a few seconds, he snatched his shirt from the floor and tugged it over his head. "It's my job," he said.

"Right."

Nice reminder. For a brief second upstairs, I thought maybe he cared about my wellbeing because I was a person.

But I was a job. Nothing more. He was getting paid well to do exactly what he'd done mere minutes ago. And he probably loved every second of manhandling the alphaholes.

I chuckled to myself at my private little joke, then shook my head at his questioning frown.

Kai tugged the bottom hem of his shirt, and I couldn't help but notice he was hiding an obvious erection.

Well then. Looked like he didn't exactly hate my scent. Or maybe it was my omega pheromones. Either way, he wasn't repulsed by me. It wasn't exactly friendship, but maybe it was something I could use to get him to stop being so distant all the time.

Or maybe…I wouldn't have to worry so much about finding a pack before my heat hit. Because from what I saw outlined by his jeans told me he could definitely get me through the worst of the cramps and fever.

And, yeah, I found myself looking forward to it a little more than I probably should have.

Kai

FUCK. My traitorous eyes refused to turn from the sight of Sophie's tight little ass swaying as she climbed the stairs.

She'd come down to talk to me and had fucking perfumed. It was like I'd been doused in flowers and caramel and I couldn't help but lick my lips in hopes of finding the taste lingering there.

No such luck.

My dick was so hard it was damned near painful. But I'd been in a state of arousal since she'd sassed me that first day. She didn't behave like other omegas I'd encountered. She wasn't meek. She wasn't shy.

And she'd been sure to shut those fuckers down when they'd tried to treat her as though she'd be nothing more than an adornment to their lives rather than a cherished member of their pack.

Her eyes had dipped when I'd done my best to cover my boner with the bottom of my shirt. I should have just pretended everything was fine. But nah, she'd seen what her nearness had done to my body.

Had she realized she'd perfumed? Had she realized her body had reacted so viscerally to mine?

It didn't matter. It didn't matter that I suddenly felt an over-whelming need to rush up the stairs after her, bend her over the nearest surface, and slam my knot so deep into her she would be ruined for any other man.

She wasn't mine. She couldn't be mine. She came from one of those families who could afford personal security for their sweet little omega daughter while a profitable and acceptable pack was found for her.

Since when did arranged relationships work? My parents sure as fuck were never happy. But those who'd found their pack organically, those who'd found their scent matches or had simply fallen in love were the ones who stayed happy.

Love. I almost laughed at myself for even thinking the word. Men like me didn't find love. We didn't find happily ever after. We worked our asses off, put ourselves in harm's way almost nightly, and often were killed on the job.

Sorrow hit hard at the thought of my two teammates who'd fallen on our last mission. They'd been using their own bodies to shield the omegas we were evacuating and had been hit and killed instantly. It wasn't until after the immediate threat was over that ORE was able to retrieve their bodies, announce their deaths to their families or packs, and give them proper burials.

That was my future. That was all I had to look forward to. And the last thing I needed to contemplate was bringing an omega – or anyone for that matter – into the mix to complicate shit further.

I needed a shower, but I wasn't quite ready to leave the basement. It was getting late, but not quite late enough for either of us to turn in. I'd lied to the pack when I'd told them she'd had another appointment, that they needed to leave.

And her feisty ass had toyed with them, teased them and asked me how many packs she should entertain. I would never admit it to her, but it had been hot as hell watching her stand up to them instead of being the sweet, obedient little omega her designation was known for, what they were expected to be.

I couldn't hide in the basement for the rest of the night. I needed to shower the sweat off – and maybe jerk off in the shower – then find out what her schedule was for the rest of the week.

As I climbed the stairs, her sweetness lingering in the stairwell did nothing to quell my need for her, to feel her wrapped around my cock, to hear her moans...

"Fuuuck," I growled as I climbed the stairs.

She was curled up on the recliner, a throw over her legs as I passed. I kept my eyes straight ahead and pretended she wasn't there, pretended I wasn't about to drown in caramel. But I could have sworn I felt her eyes burning into my back as I made the short trip to my bedroom that was across the hall from hers.

The door slammed behind me a little harder than I'd intended and I winced. How the fuck was I supposed to get my shit under control when I could still smell her perfume clinging to my skin like it had sunk into one of my many tattoos, as though it was trying to burrow itself into my skin?

Ripping my shirt over my head, I dropped it into the hamper as I passed, then shoved my jeans down over my hips. I'd wear them again tomorrow. Not like I was worried about impressing anyone.

Or, at least, I wasn't originally. I wasn't as of ten minutes ago. Now?

Damn it. No. No matter how pretty she was, no matter how edible she smelled, she couldn't and wouldn't be mine. Her mouth alone would drive me nuts. Every time she thought I so much as looked in her direction she snapped some comment or another at me.

Yeah, she was sassy, but she definitely had a chip on her shoulder.

Could I blame her, though? I couldn't imagine how it must have felt for her going through life having every step dictated simply because of her designation. I couldn't imagine having alphas sniffing after me, wanting me for nothing more than my biology and what my body had to offer.

Eh…I supposed I wouldn't mind if Sophie wanted me for that reason. If our lives were different.

She wanted a pack. Not only did I not have one, I didn't *want* one. I didn't want the risk of severing the connection if I was killed on the job. I didn't want to risk the pain those I loved would endure when they got the knock on the door that I would never return home again.

The pipes squealed as the water rushed through. Steam rose in the air, doing nothing to wash her scent from my nose.

I needed to scrub every inch of my body until it was pink or there was no way I would end up getting any sleep.

Water pounded tile and sluiced down my body, loosening tight muscles as images of Sophie flashed behind my closed lids. How would she look under the spray? How would her long blonde hair look clinging in wet strands to her thin body?

How would she sound if I took her hard and fast against the tiled wall?

With a groan, I wrapped my fist around my cock and pulled, grunting as I stroked it fast, using my other hand to squeeze my knot.

It only took seconds to spill onto the shower floor, biting my lip to keep the sounds of my release from travelling through the walls and to Sophie's ears.

CHAPTER 3

Sophie

Three. That was how many packs who'd come to meet me. And that was the number of strike outs. The second pack were far better than the first. They were polite. They'd asked simple questions, nothing like the first who'd asked about my heat.

They'd also been handsome and successful and lived near my family's home. But there was just something missing. I had never been one of those women who preferred bad boys, but there was literally no passion to any of them, nothing that made me want to cross the room and straddle their laps or bury my face against their necks to bring their scents into my lungs.

The third pack…

Kai was still pissy about that one.

There had been six men who'd crowded into the living room of the house. Why all six had come at once instead of two or three was beyond me. They'd talked over me. They'd leered. They'd done as the first and asked about my cycle.

They'd asked how many pups I wanted and how soon I was willing to start trying for a family.

And then they'd asked whether I would be willing to change my hair. Because, apparently, blondes appeared daft in the eyes of their peers.

I all but told them to get the fuck out.

"Is there something wrong with me?" I pouted as I curled up on the reclining chair.

Kai turned a frown on me. "Wrong how?"

"Why am I getting the…rejects? Am I really so old as to not deserve better?"

"Not rich enough for you?" he grumbled, turning his attention back to the movie he was watching.

"Why the hell would that be the first question on your mind? What part of any of these meetings made you think I was looking for a rich pack?"

"They're all rich. You can't tell me you didn't notice. And hate to break it to you, princess, but all omegas don't generally get to sit with private security while packs come sniffing after them in hopes of being chosen."

"Stop calling me princess," I said, trying to put as much growl into my voice as he always did.

Slowly, he turned and sat up, facing me. "Admit it – you're spoiled. Mommy and daddy are handpicking the cream of the crop just for you. And all you have to do is sit here and look pretty. You're practically thumbing through a catalogue. You have all the power and you're pretending as though you're the victim."

"Oh, excuse me! I wasn't aware it was such a privilege to have a bunch of alphas asking about my body, about my heat cycle, and telling me I'm not pretty enough for their social circle."

I'd pushed to my feet without thought and moved until I was practically standing between his knees, jabbing my finger down at him.

"You have no idea what it's like. You're a fucking alpha. You snap you fingers and get anything you want."

When Kai slowly unfolded himself from the couch until he was towering over me, I resisted the urge to either back away or lean into him.

"And you're a spoiled princess who expects perfection to walk through that door and give you a fairy tale life."

Anger flared hot, and my hand whipped through the air before I could stop it. My palm stung as it made contact with his cheek. And the jerk barely flinched from the contact.

"That is the one and only shot you get, princess. The next time you raise your hand to me, I'll put you over my knee and spank your ass pink."

"You wouldn't fucking dare."

Here I was thinking Kai was on my side, that he was growling on my behalf, that he was as angered by the line of questioning from these packs. And the whole time he saw me as nothing more than a petulant child.

"This is probably a really good time for you to walk away...princess."

I didn't bother with an open hand slap this time. I balled up my fist and aimed right for his mouth. A busted lip would definitely keep him from flapping his gums anymore.

Except...my fist never made contact. He caught it in his hand, turned me and leaned me over the arm of the couch, and did exactly as he'd promised.

The first strike to my ass caught me off guard, pulling a surprised and appalled shriek from my lips.

The next one...

The next one sent heat rushing through my veins until my panties grew damp with slick.

I couldn't bite back the moan on the third one, especially when his hand stilled on the cheek he'd assaulted, stroking it as though soothing away the sting.

His scent engulfed me, surrounded me like a blanket, warming me from head to toe, invaded my every sense and pushing away all logical thought.

When he was no longer crowding me, I straightened and slowly turned, my eyes wide as they settled on his face.

There was no way he couldn't smell what that spanking had done, how he'd awakened a hunger deep inside of me that wouldn't go away on its own.

We crashed together, his arms wrapping around my back and crushing me to his chest the same time I jumped and wrapped my arms around his neck. Our mouths slanted, teeth bumping, and then his tongue was invading my mouth, teasing and dancing and punishing my own.

Holy hell. He not only smelled like heaven, he tasted like home. He tasted like warmth and hope and happiness.

One of his arms slid down my back until it was under my ass, lifting me. I wrapped my legs around his waist, and held on as he dropped back onto the couch with me straddling his hips, rubbing and gyrating against him, trying to make contact with his hard cock through his jeans and my sleep pants.

Too many clothes. Not enough skin.

Reaching between us, I fumbled with the button and zipper of his pants, then reached inside and wrapped my fingers around his thick cock, pulling it free and stroking it in long, slow pulls. His growl was like a vibrator in all the right places, causing my nipples to pebble and ache to be touched.

Kai grabbed the sides of my pants and started to tug. I had to practically stand on the couch for him to pull them over my ass until there was no longer any barriers between us.

Sliding my sex along his length, I coated him in my slick, humming my pleasure each time my clit bumped against his swollen knot.

I didn't ask permission. I didn't question my own logic; simply reached between us so I could hold him steady and lower onto him, taking his dick inch by inch until it was fully seated in my soaked and fluttering cunt.

How the hell was I so close to coming already? We'd been fighting seconds ago. I had hit him. He had spanked me, called me spoiled. He thought I felt I was better than he was, and I thought he was a bully.

Yet my body responded to him as though he was home, as though he was built specifically to fill me the way he was now.

His hand gripped my ass and urged me to move. I didn't need the urging. I needed him. I needed friction. I needed to feel every inch of this alpha filling me.

I needed his knot.

It had nothing to do with hindbrain, nothing to do with biology. It was simply want, simply desire.

Simply pure and unadulterated lust.

My hands were on his shoulders as I rose and fell on his cock, moaning and mewling as I climbed the side of the cliff, every inch of my body tingling and sensitive and needing release.

Kai leaned forward and buried his face between my breasts before turning his head and sucking on one nipple through my tank top, dampening my shirt.

"Oh…oh shit," I cried out as my body tightened and my pussy clenched as the first ripples exploded through me.

I pushed down, trying to take his knot, trying to fill myself completely. But his hands stilled me, kept me from taking what I wanted most.

Moments later, Kai clamped his lips on my shoulder and sucked hard as he grunted, his hips pushing up hard, but not hard enough to seat his knot, merely pushing and rubbing it against my clit until another ripple of pleasure followed on the heels of the first.

By the time the aftershocks slowed and I could catch my breath, I felt dizzy. Almost like I was outside of my body and watching everything from above.

Holy shit. I'd just fucked my bodyguard when I was supposed to be courting chosen packs.

Kai

Son of a fuck.

Standing, I kept Sophie cradled against me, her legs still wrapped around me, and kicked out of my jeans so I could get us to the shower without tripping and dropping her.

What the hell had I done? I'd been teasing her about spanking her like a petulant child. But at the mention, her perfume had lifted on the air until I'd felt drunk.

And then she'd moaned and her slick had soaked her panties when my hand hit her ass over and over. She'd liked it. She'd liked my hand striking her ass.

We'd crashed together like fucking freight trains; no thought, no seconds to wonder if we were making a mistake. It was nothing short of carnal need. Primal instinct.

She'd wanted my knot. She'd tried to push down onto it, her cunt nearly sucking me into her. But I couldn't do that. It was bad enough I'd come inside of her. It wasn't my right to knot an unbonded omega who was actively seeking a pack of alphas for her life mates.

What the fuck would her parents think if they found out what we'd done? I'd end up fired. She'd end up in the care of someone else.

That thought alone caused a growl to rumble up my chest as I walked us into the shower and turned on the spray, my back to the water so she wouldn't be pelted with freezing cold water.

"Unwrap your legs," I said, just short of a bark.

With a frustrated groan, she unhooked her legs and slid down my body, her slick coated pussy rubbing against my once more hardening cock.

I couldn't shower in here with her. That would be a mistake. If I stayed with her, if I watched her soapy hands roam her body, I would lose my mind and take her again. And again. Until neither of us could stand.

Helping her pull her tank over her head, I cursed again.

"What?" she asked, her cheeks growing pink as she raised her arms to cover herself. Yup. She was feeling the same regret and shame I felt.

Pushing her hair over her shoulder, I stared at the growing hickey I'd left when I'd filled her pussy.

"I left a hickey on your shoulder." I ran my finger over it and bit the inside of my cheek when the desire to sink my teeth into that exact spot nearly took my breath.

She turned her head to try for a better look. With a shrug, she kicked her pants the rest of the way off and stepped under the spray. "I can cover it with makeup or clothing until it heals."

Because she still had to look appealing to prospective packs. She would continue entertaining alphas, would continue considering them for courting.

Turning on my heel, I left her to shower alone and headed for my own room.

"Fuck," I gritted out, barely containing the bellow of…what? Rage? Jealousy? Shame?

I felt all of them. I wanted to despise Sophie. I wanted to despise the fact I was stuck in this house with her instead of doing my job. I wanted to hate her for the way she found something wrong with every pack that had visited her thus far.

Although even I could admit two of the groups had been dicks. Change her hair? Really? She was gorgeous. She was a natural honey blonde, the length almost to her waist when she didn't spend time curling it. She always wore makeup when the alphas showed up, but I knew what she looked like when she woke up in the morning. I knew how she looked with bed mussed hair and a bare face, her pretty freckles on full display, her thin but obviously kissable lips devoid of lipstick or gloss.

I didn't hate her. I didn't despise her. I despised the fuckers who actually had a chance with someone like Sophie. They were the alphas parents wanted for their sweet, fragile omegas.

Sophie wasn't fragile. She'd proven that. She was a hellcat. She'd taken my cock like a champ, ridden me until she'd found what she sought and fallen apart with the most beautiful moan, her lips parting as she cried out.

I definitely felt shame. I wasn't ashamed that I'd had sex with someone as beautiful as Sophie, but that I'd fucked her on the couch while still half dressed. I would have rather we'd been naked. I would have rather we'd been stretched out on the bed so I could have taken my time tasting her and making her come over and over on my tongue before giving her my dick.

Or letting her take what she wanted and needed from me.

Turning the spray on in my own bathroom, I cursed my body as my dick began to harden again. Once would never be enough with someone like Sophie. Especially after feeling the way she clenched around me as she fell apart.

As I'd done every fucking day since getting a whiff of Sophie's perfume, I wrapped my hand around my cock and jerked off, spilling onto the shower stall to be washed down the drain with the rest. If the urban legend had been true, I would have been blind by now.

Once would never be enough. But it would have to be. It couldn't happen again. I had nothing to offer Sophie except a mate who worked late nights, who held a dangerous job, and who could leave her a widow.

She deserved more. The princess deserved her prince. She deserved her castle. No matter how much I teased her about it, she deserved to be treated like royalty.

A smile teased my lips as I tried to imagine any one of those alphas who'd shown up trying to deal with an omega who not only spoke her mind but had no problem taking what she wanted from her alpha. And, whether she'd known before tonight or not, my sweet, sassy, beautiful omega liked her ass spanked.

Dick rising again, I couldn't help but wonder what other kinks I could discover if I had the time.

But I wouldn't have that chance. I would have to keep my distance, watch over her as I was hired to do, keep her safe, and watch her walk away when she found the pack right for her.

CHAPTER 4

Sophie

It had been a week since the last time any packs had contacted my parents to request a meeting with me. It had also been a week since Kai and I had screwed on the couch.

In that week, he'd done just about everything he could to keep distance between us. He rarely sat in the living room while I watched TV, instead retreating to his bedroom or the basement to pummel the punching bag or lift weights.

What the hell had I been thinking?

That was the problem – I *hadn't* been thinking. I'd reacted. My hindbrain had taken over. My body had reacted to his scent, his nearness, the sting of his hand on my ass, then the smoothing of his palm along the marks he'd left.

It was obvious he'd enjoyed himself, but now he obviously regretted it. Not that he'd said as much…or really anything in the past seven days more than the grunts and two-word answers like the first day I'd moved in here.

An annoying chirp sounded from my bedroom. With a huff, I pushed to my feet and jogged barefoot to where I'd left my phone. There was no reason to carry it around. The only people who called me were my parents. And that was only to either let me know of another appointment or ask how one of the meetings went.

"Hello?" I asked on the fourth ring, my breathing a little rapid from running to answer.

"What's wrong with you?" my dad asked. One of my dads. Since all my mom's alphas looked amusingly similar, I'd never been sure which had actually sired me. But they'd all raised us in a similar fashion, like they were all our fathers, and trained my sister, brother, and me in the way they'd trained my omega mother – to be subservient to her alphas.

That lesson had never really sunk into my brain or heart. I couldn't picture myself letting someone boss me around or make decisions for my life without my input.

But wasn't I? Wasn't I doing exactly that as I stayed locked in the house with Kai while my family decided who was suitable enough to meet with me?

"Nothing. Why?"

"You're out of breath." His tone was suspicious.

The temptation to tell him I'd been busy knocking boots was strong, but that would do nothing but cause a fight. And possibly get Kai in trouble.

"I left my phone in the bedroom. I had to run to answer it. What's up?"

"Only two applicants this week," Dad said. Growing up, they'd each had nicknames. Because it got confusing when there were four men who would answer to the same name. This one was Jim. Or Daddy Jim, as I'd called him as a child. "I'm not getting the best feedback from those you've met with."

Plopping onto the side of the bed, I laid backward and stared up at the ceiling. "What kind of feedback?"

Papers rustled and I could picture him leaning over his desk, reading printouts instead of simply reading the emails he'd more than likely been sent. "Argumentative. Unwilling to receive constructive criticism. Rude. Unreceptive to alpha's compliments. Unwilling to discuss breeding schedules."

I wrinkled my nose as I continued staring at the stark white ceiling. "They were jerks, Dad. One said I was too old and had small... breasts." I omitted the actual word the first jerk had used. "One repeatedly asked about my heat cycle – "

"That's normal. They need to know whether you're fertile. At your age, the window is closing quickly and there might not be a point to courting you if you're unable to carry pups."

"I'm not even thirty, Dad. I have plenty of time. Another of the assholes said I should change my hair because I wouldn't fit in with his social circle."

"You would look nice with darker hair."

"There is nothing wrong with my hair, Dad. Mom has blonde hair. Do you think *she* should dye it brown?"

He hummed but didn't respond to my question.

"Is there something going on between you and your security? One of your suitors seemed to believe the guard watched you too closely. He said he growled several times."

"He's supposed to watch over me. And he growled when they asked rude and personal questions on the very first meeting."

"Maybe we should have you moved. Or hire a new guard," he said, his tone almost distracted.

"No!" I said too loudly and too quickly. "I mean, then I would have to get used to a new person all over again. It's awkward enough having someone in the room when I'm talking to these packs. I don't want to have to do it in front of another stranger. Kai's fine. He's keeping me safe. He has no personal interest in me past his job."

My heart began to race as the silence stretched. There was no way he could know that I'd practically ravaged Kai on the couch, that I'd tried to force myself onto his knot. But the longer the silence stretched, the tighter my nerves coiled.

"I'll text you the schedule for the week. But I suggest doing more to be more accepting of the packs. Try to find the good instead of only looking for the bad. These alphas have the means to keep you in the life you're accustomed. You'll be able to raise your pups in comfort."

"I just want someone to want me for me, Dad. I don't want a pack who is more focused on my heat cycle instead of getting to know me. Not one of them has asked about my education, about my hobbies, or even asked for a date. They just show up at the house and pepper me with uncomfortable questions."

"And you'll answer those questions. If they're a match, you all can get to know each other later." More rustling of papers. "The first pack only has four alphas, but they're in higher levels of government. So even when they're not home, you'll have personal security. The second pack has eight alphas—"

"Eight?!" I all but squawked. "Not all eight are interested in me, though, right?"

It wasn't exactly unheard of for an omega to have a larger pack. But that wasn't what I wanted. I would be just as happy with two alphas. Or even an alpha and a beta. Eight alphas were a lot of men who would be vying for my attention and my body on a regular basis.

"Yes, Sophia Elizabeth. Eight. Finance, law enforcement, and two who work for my firm. That is the only reason I was able to get this group to apply at all. We're running out of prospects. Word is getting around about how difficult you are."

Anger turned my stomach. Running out of prospects. There were so many people on this planet. So many alphas. So many betas. Yet he was only counting those whom he and my other dads felt were adequate to court and mate with their omega daughter.

Why was it so hard for them to simply want the best for me? Why couldn't they be happy with an alpha who wanted to love me as I was, to want to dote on me and cherish me because they loved me and not because they were *supposed* to or because it was custom.

"The pack of eight understands it might be a little overwhelming, so only two will meet at the house. The group of four have requested an outing. After hearing of the difficulties you've had with the others, they think a change of scenery might be best."

"They want to actually take me on a date before meeting me?"

Okay, that didn't sound as bad. The others acted as though they were interviewing me to decide whether they wanted to court me. At least these guys were thinking ahead, thinking of my needs instead of what they wanted from me.

"I'll text the dates and times when they're all finalized. Do you need more clothing? You mother said she made sure you brought decent dresses, but I can send over more if you need."

"I have enough." Especially since I'd been living in lounge clothes every day that I wasn't meeting with prospective packs. "But thank you," I added on.

I wanted to believe Jim and the others were doing what they felt was best for me. It wasn't exactly safe for an unbonded omega to be out and about among alphas. A claim was at least a barrier against rutting alphas, or even horny betas.

A sigh ruffled over the line. "Just...give them a chance. Listen to what they have to say. I'm running out of favors."

Sitting up quickly, my brows slammed together. Favors? Was my dad asking these people to take his spinster omega off his hands? I wasn't even in the house anymore. Why the hell did he care whether I was packed up or not?

Although, he was paying for the housing and the personal security. But only because he'd refused to let me actually get a job after I'd finished school and received my degree.

"Send me the schedule. I'll talk to you later."

He ended the call without anything else spoken. No declarations of love. No well wishes. I wasn't sure I'd ever heard the word love uttered in my family.

Honestly, I wasn't sure whether I'd ever known what real love was, how it felt. I assumed my mom loved us, but her life had been so centered around her alphas that we were almost always pushed off on our nannies to be tended to.

With a frustrated huff, I tossed the phone back onto the nightstand and decided on a long, hot bubble bath. I needed to relax, loosen the muscles that had grown tight since I'd seen the name on the caller ID.

Kai

EIGHT FUCKING ALPHAS. Sophie's dad had set up a meeting for a pack with eight fucking alphas. One omega and eight alphas.

What the fuck was he thinking? Even if they were some kind of a match, her first heat in a house with eight alphas could end up in a rutting mess. That was dangerous as hell.

But I had literally no say in the matter. My opinion meant shit. And she was obviously not overly happy with me these days. Especially since I'd done everything in my power to keep distance between us after feeling her wrapped and clenching around my cock.

It wasn't that I didn't want to be near her. It was the exact opposite. The more her scent burrowed its way into my senses, the closer I wanted to get. And the more I wanted to feel her under my hands. My tongue. Wrapped around my knot.

We hadn't even gotten fucking naked. I hadn't even seen her perky little tits. I'd teased her nipple through the tank, had watched as they'd pebbled against the thin material when she'd straddled me and sunk onto my dick.

But I hadn't run my hands over her small body. Hadn't tasted the sweetness of her slick. And that was exactly why I couldn't be in the same room with her for more than a few minutes at a time. I didn't know whether she was aware, but every time I was near, she perfumed. And that shit was going to send me into a mindless rut.

Knotting her and marking her would be the fastest way to lose my fucking job.

Sophie was currently in her bedroom getting ready for a date. One of the packs had requested to take her to dinner for their first meeting rather than crowding into the house. Which didn't sit well with me. Too much could go wrong. There would be more people to watch, more exits and entries to keep an eye on. At least this pack only contained four alphas.

But my job was to do as I was told, and that included escorting her to some ritzy ass restaurant uptown. Which meant I had to dress accordingly.

I'd donned a pair of black slacks, a black button up shirt, black tie, and a black jacket. And had to actually trim up my beard and run a comb through my hair.

I felt more like I was heading to a job as a fucking maître d' than acting as security. But standing out could be as much of a risk as blending into the patrons of the place.

Sitting on the couch, my knee bobbed as I stared off into space and waited for the princess to exit so we could head off to meet with her princes.

I'd started calling her princess as a jab. But for some reason, the title stuck. She kind of was a princess. Or at least pretty enough to be one.

The door to her bedroom opened and she stepped into the living room, her heels clacking against the hardwood floor a second before she rounded the corner. She wore a dress that hugged her thin but shapely body like a glove. The dress dipped a little in the front, giving only a hint of cleavage. Her hair was loose and perfectly waved down to her hips, swaying a little as she walked.

She didn't wear makeup around the house. I'd grown used to her pretty freckles, her thin but kissable lips.

Tonight, her eyes were smokey and dark, her lips shined with gloss. And those freckles I'd grown fond of were all but gone under the crap women wore on their faces.

Her hands were raised as she clipped an earring into her right ear, a handbag tucked under her left arm.

"Ready?" she asked.

When her eyes rose to me, she stilled, then her arms slowly dropped to her sides.

I pushed to my feet and let my eyes roam her from head to toe, avoiding the urge to reach down and shift my growing cock. Fuck, she was gorgeous. I preferred her natural. I preferred her pretty face without the makeup, her hair hanging loose or even in the messy knot she tended to wear around the house.

But this? She was practically a wet fucking dream right in front of me.

Sticky sweetness swamped the room, and I jerked my eyes to her face. Her pupils were blown, her lips were parted as she took deep breaths, and her nipples strained against the material of her dress.

Fuuuck.

Clearing my throat, I turned and opened the front door, holding it for her as I stepped outside. I needed space between us. I needed fresh air before I locked us inside and ripped that dress from her body so I could finally see every inch of her naked body.

It was a few more seconds before Sophie stepped out. Her shoulders were back, her chin was raised, and she kept her eyes straight ahead as she walked beside me to my waiting SUV.

She wasn't mine, but that didn't stop the manners that had been instilled in me. I opened her door and waited until she was situated and buckled before swinging it shut.

And I might have taken a few extra seconds to get my head straight and gulp in fresh air before I was locked in the cab with her pheromones teasing me the entire ride to the restaurant.

"You look nice," I said into the quiet as I aimed the vehicle out of the suburbs and toward downtown.

"Thank you. So do you," she said.

Neither of us looked in the other's direction. After a few minutes, I couldn't take it anymore and reached forward, turning the radio on, then cracked my window. I needed a physical distraction and needed to at least subdue her perfume. She should have applied scent blocker. Because she was going to drive every alpha in the place crazy the second she stepped inside.

Fuck. That was going to make my job all that much harder. I might not only have the pack she was meeting to contend with; there could be dozens of unbonded alphas in the place and they would all be eying my omega.

Not my omega. My assignment. I would have to repeat that over and over in my head; remind my heart, mind, and dick that this beautiful woman was on the hunt for a pack of her own.

The parking lot was full, which didn't bode well for my fears of a perfuming omega in public with no pack bonds.

Taking a deep breath, I shoved my handgun into the back of my pants before settling my jacket over it and ignored her gaping before stepping out of the SUV and rounding the hood.

She slid her hand into mine and allowed me to help her from her seat, holding on to me for another second while she gave her ankles time to stabilize in the torture devices she wore on her feet.

I never understood why women would put themselves through wearing those things, but even I could admit she looked fucking amazing. And I sure as fuck wouldn't have any qualms with her being naked and spread out before me with those sexy ass strappy shoes still on her feet.

Biting back a growl, I breathed through my mouth and tried to focus on my surroundings as we stepped inside and Sophie gave her name.

"Your party is here. This way," the hostess said, leading the way to a table near the back.

A few familiar faces smiled at me as I passed. Members of ORE out with their omega. At least if shit went sideways, I would have a little backup. It put my mind at ease a little more but did nothing to erase the need tightening my body as I watched Sophie walk in front of me.

Eyes on the crowd and off her ass.

Four alphas rose from the table and introduced themselves, taking her hand in turn and placing a light kiss to the back of her hand.

Okay. This was a lot better than the assholes who'd met with her so far. They were at least behaving as gentlemen.

Stepping away from the table, I plastered my back to a wall where I could see Sophie, her prospective pack, as well as the rest of the room. I clasped my hands in front of me, kept my senses on alert, and listened in to the table as they began light conversation, suggesting they order drinks or dinner before the interview process.

Interview? Really?

But that was exactly how every single meeting had felt thus far, like they were interviewing Sophie for a position in their pack rather than learning about this beautiful woman. I'd barely spent just over a week with her and already I found myself wanting to know more. I wanted to know why she was obviously resistant to packing up. I wanted to know how she'd gone so long without claiming an alpha. I wanted to know why she was so fucking sassy and argumentative instead of timid like other omegas I'd met.

Maybe she was like the omega sitting with the ORE members. Maybe she'd presented later in life and had lived her life as a beta. That would definitely explain her resistance to living her life as an obedient little omega.

Honestly, if I were to ever want an omega, if I were to ever decide pack life was for me, she was exactly the kind of woman I would want in my life. No doubt she would do everything she could to put me in my place any time I displeased her.

And I would enjoy pinking her ass again every time she sassed me.

CHAPTER 5

Sophie

$\mathcal{I}$'d made sure Kai knew the kind of place where we would dine tonight, and hoped he owned more than the jeans and tees I'd seen him wear day in and day out.

But I hadn't expected him to look so damn yummy when I'd stepped out of my room. My brain had turned to mush and my panties had grown damp. The way he'd stared at me and the way his dick had instantly hardened let me know I'd filled the room with my scent.

All I could hope was that it would be more contained when I was sitting with the new prospective pack. I didn't want them thinking I was primed and ready for them. Or that I was in heat. They would immediately agree to bond me if they thought I was ready to spread my legs and beg for their knots. Hindbrain was a hell of a thing.

"Your father told us you have a master's degree," Chris said. For once, I remembered their names. Probably because they actually spent time trying to get to know me instead of asking the usual, boring, and embarrassing questions.

Chris, Anton, Eric, and Brian. Normal names. Handsome faces. Pleasant but subdued scents. And they were all paying attention to me instead of staring at any part of my body that wasn't hidden by the table.

"I do. Masters in Omega Social Services. I'd planned on one day opening a facility to aid unbonded omegas in navigating society."

Chris nodded, his brows high. "The Omega Center has been helpful."

"The Omega Center helps omegas find packs. They help with education. And, at times, help with suppressants and birth control. I want to one day have a center that will help them not only live among alphas without the risk of being claimed against their will," I made sure to look each of them in the eye as I spoke to gauge their reaction to my statements, "but to find fulfilling jobs and become equal members of society. There is no reason an omega can't run for government or even act as law enforcement."

"Until their cycle hits," Eric said. His words were even, but there was something in his eye, something that didn't sit right.

He was closest to me, sitting to my right. Anton was on my left. Brian and Chris were across from me.

"That is where suppressants come in. I would like to lobby congress for further studies to find safe alternatives since we don't yet know the effects of long-term use of suppressants. If one was found, omegas would have more control over their lives."

"Interesting," Brian said with a nod. "You believe with the right suppressants omegas would be able to skirt their cycles?"

"Yes. Exactly. If we could avoid the cycle, we wouldn't require the time spent hidden away while our bodies are taken over by our hormones, while pain and fever wreak havoc on our bodies."

They nodded politely but offered nothing to the conversation. Which told me they either doubted my beliefs that we could be productive members of society or that we should stick to the rules set by nature. I didn't like either of those choices.

"Have you lobbied anyone yet?" Brian finally asked. He nodded to the waiter as drinks were set on the table.

I'd decided against dinner for now, at least until I decided whether I wanted to spend much time with these guys. It was going well at first, but now, I wasn't so sure.

"I haven't. I had barely finished my degree when my dads…" I cleared my throat and took a sip from my dirty martini. "I suppose I'll have to wait to see what my future pack thinks of my plans."

The men exchanged a look that I couldn't decipher. Hopefully, they weren't high fiving themselves just yet. They smelled nice, but their scents did nothing even close to what Kai's did to my body. I wanted to know that whoever I was stuck with for the rest of my life was someone who could not only hold an intelligent conversation with me, that their scents would awaken a hunger inside of me, but would also support my goals and dreams for my future.

Thus far, none of the alphas looked as though they liked the idea of an independent omega.

"I hate to ask such personal questions," Anton started, "but do you desire a family? Is motherhood something you see for your future?"

Another sip of my martini. Nodding, I set the glass down and folded my hands in my lap. "Yes. Someday. I don't see why I can't raise children and build something that could change society. At least for omegas."

"You're twenty-eight?" Anton asked.

"Yes."

And here came the part of the conversation where I knew this pack wasn't it for me.

"I suppose there is time to do both. You're still young."

I stared at Anton. Blinked. Blinked again. Holy crap. Not what I had expected him to say. These men weren't like the others my father had sent sniffing after me. They genuinely seemed interested in me. And so far, they weren't showing doubt about my choices in my future nor were they making it obvious they would expect me to stay home, barefoot and pregnant, while they lived their lives.

"Is funding an issue, or is it simply the timing?" Brian asked.

"What?"

"If funding for your project is an issue, I'm sure we can help. Or if you were simply waiting to find a pack…"

I looked at each man in turn, then downed the rest of my martini before signaling to the waiter for another.

"I, uh…I hadn't gotten that far in planning. I literally received my degree six months before my dad… You would help me with the funding? And the planning?"

"I don't see why our omega would need to ask for outside help."

"Well, I'm not your omega."

"*Yet*," Eric teased.

A hand touched my knee under the table and I jumped.

A soft growl rattled from behind me. I knew it was from Kai. So did the other four.

Eric's hand slowly retreated and he looked over his shoulder at the guard who had shadowed me on every meeting since the first day.

"I think what Eric is trying to say is we're interested in courting you. If you're amenable to that," Anton said, his pretty blue eyes twinkling with amusement as he shook his head at his packmate.

"I, uh…" Of the groups I'd met, these four were probably the closest to acceptable in my mind. They seemed supportive of my goals. They weren't rattling on about me breeding. They hadn't asked the cringey questions about my heat and hadn't batted an eye when I'd mentioned using heat suppressants or that I wanted to wait to have pups.

The scent of burned cookies met my nose. Kai. His scent had turned a little bitter, a little charred. Why? Other than Eric's hand on my knee, none of these guys had done anything untoward nor had they asked anything that would make me uncomfortable.

Shouldn't he be happy? He would be free of me. He would no longer have to avoid me every minute of the day.

There would still be the courting period, so we would be stuck together for a while. But then he could go about his life and return to whatever job he did when he wasn't babysitting omegas.

"I would be amenable," I said, a slow smile stretching across my face as the men grinned at me, looks of joy obvious all around.

KAI HAD BEEN EVEN MORE quiet than normal since that night at the restaurant. He refused to look me in the eye and was practically invisible. He no longer waited for me to enter a room before he vacated it; he was simply missing every day, either beating the crap out of the bag downstairs, watching TV in his bedroom, or sitting at the table on the back patio.

He was doing his job, I supposed, but I was...well, lonely. Which was silly. Not like the two of us spent hours conversing. It was tense and awkward after I'd climbed him like a tree then took from his body what I craved.

Now, it was downright creepy. He behaved like he was the secret service, like his presence should be known but not seen.

Whether he stayed away or not, I was fully aware of him, fully aware of his warm, sweet scent that had permeated every square inch of the house we shared.

Tonight was the first night Anton and his pack started their courtship. They'd invited me over to their home for dinner. Unfortunately – whether for Kai, myself, or the guys – proper ladies brought up in affluent and influential households didn't go to an alpha's house unchaperoned. Meaning Kai would be tagging along once more.

In the two-minute conversation we'd had over coffee before he'd stepped onto the back deck, I let him know the plans and told him he didn't need to bother with the suit and tie again. It was casual. Well, casual for him. I would still have to keep up appearances, still dress to impress.

But at least I wouldn't have to pretend to be someone I wasn't. The pack had appeared intrigued by my ideas for an organization with the sole intent of furthering education and protecting omegas who chose to live unbonded and unclaimed by an alpha or pack.

He waited by the door as I hopped through the living room, slipping my feet into flats this time instead of heels. I'd chosen a pair of straight-leg jeans and a blouse that dipped low in the back, tied around the neck, then opened almost completely in the back. Which meant, of course, that I couldn't wear a bra without looking tacky.

I didn't plan on revealing so much skin all night, though. Unless the night went well, of course.

Tugging my arms through a blazer, I then pulled my hair from the collar and checked the wavy strands in the reflection of the darkened television screen.

"Do I look like I'm trying too hard?" I asked Kai, although I wasn't sure why or what I expected him to say.

"You look pretty," he said, barely brushing me with a glance. There was no slow perusal of my body the way he'd done when I'd worn that dress and heels the first night I'd met the pack. And his hands were cupped in front of him so I couldn't tell whether my outfit and appearance had at least provoked a boner.

I hadn't regretted sleeping with Kai, not at first, but the longer he went acting as though I was nothing but a paycheck and almost a nuisance, the more ashamed I was that I'd practically thrown myself at him and offered my body on a silver platter.

Not that he'd fought me off. Not that he'd attempted to stop me other than preventing me from dropping onto his knot. And he'd left a bruise on my shoulder, a hickey, like a temporary little mark when he'd gotten off.

Whatever. I would simply chalk it up to a one-night-stand. It had been good. I'd gotten off, too. I'd enjoyed myself. And now, it would stay as nothing more than a memory.

I had four men who were waiting for me, who wanted to spend time getting to know me, who wanted to court me in hopes of bringing me into their pack.

Kai was silent the entire drive to an area a few neighborhoods from where my parents lived. It was a far cry from the house the two of us had been sharing. It was as big and opulent as my parents, complete with the security gate wrapping the property.

"Safe," Kai muttered as he pulled up to the gate and hit the call button.

The gates swung inward, allowing Kai to pull the SUV forward and down the long, perfectly smooth driveway where Chris, Bryan, Anton, and Eric waited with open, warm smiles on their faces. They were casually dressed in jeans and button-down shirts, similar to the way Kai had dressed, and made me glad I hadn't chosen a flashy dress.

"Should we come up with some signal?" Kai grumbled as he put the vehicle in park.

"For what?" I pulled my eyes from the waiting pack to look at my personal bodyguard.

"If you want to leave. Or someone makes you uncomfortable."

He wasn't looking at me. He wasn't even looking in my direction. He was practically glaring at the men watching and waiting for me to join them for dinner.

"I'm sure it'll be fine. If they make me uncomfortable, I'll let them know. If I want to leave, I'll say so. In case you haven't noticed, I don't have a difficult time speaking my mind."

He huffed a sound that sounded almost like a laugh before pushing from the driver's seat.

"Evergreen," I said quickly, giving him a code word before he could close the door. No reason not to have a plan in place.

Eric hurried forward and pulled my door open, offering a hand and escorting me up the few concrete stairs to the landing in front of the house.

"You have a beautiful home," I said, and smiled as they all but preened at my compliment.

"Thank you," Eric said as he stepped in ahead of me and waited as we all filed through the door with Kai bringing up the rear.

"Can I get you something to drink, Mister..." Bryan started and waited for Kai to fill in the rest.

"Kai. Just Kai. And no thank you," he replied, following us to the dining room where he practically slunk into the shadows to keep watch while staying inconspicuous. As if a man his size could disappear.

"How about you, Sophia?" Bryan said.

"Sophie. And a glass of red wine would be great. Thank you."

Bryan dipped his head and left the room. When he returned, he carried several glasses and a bottle of Merlot. Anton held out a chair for me and waited until I sat before claiming a seat at the head of the table to my right. Bryan sat across from me. Eric sat on my left with Chris taking the fourth chair at the foot of the table. It was obvious they'd removed leaves from the table to make it cozier for our little dinner party. The room was large enough for a table that fit twenty. It was also decorated in a similar fashion as my parents', only less pretentious. It was like they were downplaying their wealth while still using items that could easily be sold for thousands of dollars a pop.

I was tempted to look back at Kai, see how he was faring surrounded by so much money, but didn't want to be rude and look as though the pack didn't have my full attention.

"Thank you," I said when Bryan poured my glass first and set it before me.

I sipped at it, savoring the rich flavor. Conversation began to flow as easily as it had back at the restaurant. By the time the first course was served, I'd had two glasses of wine and was beginning to feel the effects. Good thing I would be putting food in my belly. The last thing I needed was to get drunk and lose all inhibitions.

These guys were good looking, polite, and, so far, on the top of my list for a pack. Actually, they were the only ones on the list. They were the only ones who didn't make me wish I was anywhere but in their presence.

As my third glass was filled, I tucked into my salad, making sure the cloth napkin was across my lap and I was taking small enough bites to maintain appearances of a well-trained and well-raised omega.

"We might have found a location for your organization," Eric said as I slipped another bite of salad between my lips.

I nearly choked on the food, swallowing hard and taking a sip of my wine before turning wide eyes on him. "You what?"

Eric looked to his packmates. "We discussed your idea with someone and might have found a brick-and-mortar location to start your organization."

"So…you would support me if I were to spend my days and nights working with and helping other omegas instead of hanging around here and playing Susie Homemaker?"

A round of deep chuckles made my cheeks warm. "You've already let us know of your future plans. We know you wish to wait to start a family. While I would prefer you at least take a little time off while we complete the bonds and then maybe a few months after our first child is born, we all support your idea."

I had to remind myself to breathe. And blink. While I might not admit it, even to myself, I kept waiting for the other shoe to drop. I kept waiting for some deep, dark secret to emerge to remind me of exactly why I'd waited so long to claim a pack of my own.

Taking another sip of wine, I racked my brain for something to say.

"I'm…at a loss for words," I admitted.

"A simple thank you works," Anton said.

For a second, his smile felt forced. It didn't reach his eyes as he watched me over his wine goblet, slowly bringing it to his lips.

"Thank you?" I squeaked out, then cleared my throat. "I mean, thank you. So much. I don't think a location is necessary just yet. There are so many things that need to happen first. But…really?"

Why couldn't I take what they were saying at face value?

Looking back at Eric, I found him watching me again, only the smile had changed. Mischievous? Flirty? Dark?

I couldn't identify it through my wine hazy brain.

I shouldn't have drank so much. I should stop now, stop the whole night before I either made a fool of myself or ruined everything by expressing my doubts. These guys were nice. They believed in my dreams. They supported my choice for my future.

Lifting the napkin, I dabbed at my lips and stood. "Could I use your powder room?" I asked.

"Of course," Eric said, standing and pulling out my chair.

Like an idiot, I swayed and shot out a hand, grabbing onto Eric's arm for balance until my legs cooperated. "This way."

He guided me down a hallway and reached around the wall to flip on the light of a bathroom that was the size of my bedroom back at my temporary home.

"Thank you," I said, closing the door and leaning against the wood while I tried to slow my heart and my thoughts.

They'd offered to invest in my business idea. They supported the fact I wanted to put motherhood and homemaking on hold so I could help as many omegas as possible and use the degree I'd worked so hard for.

They were attractive. They were financially well off. And my parents obviously approved of them.

So what was giving me pause? Why was I doing my damnedest to find skeletons in the closet?

One name bounced around in my head. *Shut up. Don't ruin this*, I chastised myself as I once more wondered what Kai thought of the house, of the situation, of the pack.

I didn't need to use the restroom but didn't want them to think I was being weird, either. After a few minutes, I flushed the toilet and then washed my hand, pressing the cool water to my cheeks and using the hand towel hanging from a brushed gold holder to dab at the water.

Eric was outside the door when I pulled it open and startled me. Slapping a hand to my chest, I giggled. "Sorry. You scared me."

He stepped closer until I would either be pressed against his body or had to retreat. Between the wine, the offer to support my future business, and the dark look in his eyes, I decided to stand my ground, even when he reached forward to wrap an arm around my waist and pull me flush to his body.

His hardness pressed against my stomach as his hand wandered under the blazer until it hit the bared skin of my back. "Your scent has been driving me crazy all night."

Because I hadn't bothered with scent blockers. As much as I wanted an alpha to desire me naturally, I also wasn't so naïve as to believe our natural biology wasn't just as important. We had to be compatible in every way, and that included our scent signatures.

Lowering his face, he dipped his nose to the base of my throat right where it met my shoulder and inhaled deeply. His free hand gripped one of my hips while the hand on my back kept me pressed to his body as close as we could get while still dressed.

"Fuck," he growled before raising his head and slanting his lips over mine.

He smelled of roasted marshmallows, just this side of burned. A little smokey, a little charred. But still sweet. He tasted sweet, too, his natural essence mixing with the Merlot as his tongue invaded my mouth, teasing and testing mine.

The smallest whimper escaped my throat, but he swallowed the sound. His hand left my hip and smoothed up the front of my body until he cupped one of my breasts, massaging it until he tweaked my pebbled nipple beneath.

No. This felt…wrong. It felt good but wrong all the same. He was a good kisser. And slick had formed between my thighs, but I didn't feel the desire to pull him into the bathroom, strip him naked, and present for him as though he truly were my alpha.

Pulling back, I gasped when he tugged at my top as though trying to reveal one or both of my breasts.

"Wait," I said, pushing at his chest.

His pupils were blown, and his erection strained against his pants. He'd better not go into rut while trapping me in the bathroom. And if he did, I just hoped Kai would be successful at getting to my side before it was too late.

"Eric, wait," I said, using his name to hopefully snap him back to reality. "We need to slow down."

His hands lowered slowly and he blinked at me a few times, taking deep breaths of air through his open mouth.

"I can smell your slicked pussy. I can smell how badly you want me," he said, his voice deep and husky.

For some reason, those words coming from Eric's mouth sounded ugly. Kind of gross. I wasn't one to shy from dirty talk, but…

Eric wasn't my alpha.

"I think I should go," I said, trying to push past him.

His hand snaked out and grabbed my arm while the other pawed at me, pushing between my thighs.

"Stop," I said, shoving at him.

The next time he reached for me, he was yanked away with enough force to land him onto his ass. And then Kai was standing in front of me, his giant body practically blocking the entire doorway.

"Time to go," Kai said over his shoulder.

My clutch was in one of his big hands and he was practically vibrating with anger. He reached behind his back and waited until I slipped my hand into his.

"What the hell is going on?" Bryan asked as he rounded the corner.

"Your packmate just attempted to sexually assault my client," Kai said, his tone nothing short of deadly.

"What did you do?" Anton asked Eric, his head tilted down and anger bright in his eyes.

"She wanted it. Smell her. I can smell her slick from here."

Kai released my hand and lunged forward, but I caught his forearm and pulled him back.

"Let's just go," I said, a whine in my words.

Strong and independent, but still an omega. And still half the size of every one of the five men crowding the hallway and crowding me.

I had to practically drag Kai from the hallway and to the door where he kept his body between mine and the four men watching us leave.

"Wait. Please. Don't judge us for the actions of this buffoon," Anton pleaded.

"I'll...I need time to think," I said. Although there wasn't much to think about.

Would Eric have forced himself on me had Kai not intervened? Would his packmates have stopped him if they'd heard him pushing me past my limit? Or would they have simply used our courtship as an excuse, said it was biology and that Eric couldn't help himself because of my scent?

I knew I hadn't perfumed. The only person who'd caused that in the past few weeks had been Kai.

He ripped the front door open and shoved me through, slamming it shut behind him. Then he was hurrying me to his SUV, hitting the fob to unlock the doors before we reached the passenger side.

Once we were both in our seatbelts and on our way back to the house, trembles started in my belly and radiated out until they settled all the way to my toes.

I had enjoyed Eric's kiss. I had enjoyed the sweetness of his mouth. Had even felt my body warm at his touch. But since I wasn't currently enslaved by my cycle and not quite drunk enough to forget my personal rules about sleeping around on the first date, I had been able to stop us from going any further. Obviously, that had angered Eric.

I still couldn't believe the entitled fucker had the gall to try to reveal my breasts. He'd touched me. He'd shoved his hand between my thighs. And once again, I was thankful I hadn't worn a dress, something that would have given him far too much access to my body.

All I wanted right now was to get home, put on some comfy clothes, and snuggle into a blanket. The nest was even more appealing, even if I wasn't in heat. I wanted comfort. I wanted…

I wanted to call my parents and tell them they could stick the whole thing up their butts, that I no longer had any desire to be packed up. For once, I thought I'd met some good guys, alphas who could control themselves. And they'd proven me wrong.

Glancing at Kai, I couldn't ignore the tick in his jaw or the way he gripped the steering wheel so tightly his knuckles were white. He was an alpha and he'd controlled himself. He might have spanked my ass, but I was the one who'd started everything, the one who'd kissed him, the one who'd yanked his pants open so I could feel skin on skin.

And he hadn't touched me since then. He'd given me space. He'd stayed out of my way. He hadn't demanded anything else from me.

As big and gruff and masculine as he was, he'd been a complete gentleman where the men who'd been raised at the top of society's ladder…

Not all of them had behaved the way Eric had. I needed to remind myself. I couldn't very well judge the entire pack based on the actions of one of their members any more than I could judge all alphas based on the behavior of a few assholes.

Hell, I was an omega and so completely opposite of my mom and my siblings. I wasn't demure. I wasn't submissive or subservient.

Thankfully, we weren't far from home. I didn't wait for Kai to round the hood, didn't wait for him to open my door. He met me on the porch, unlocking the door and pushing it open when I practically shouldered my way in.

I needed out of these clothes. I needed the burned marshmallow smell as far from me as possible. I needed soft and cozy.

Hurrying through the dark house, I didn't bother closing the bedroom door behind me as I started yanking the blazer down my arms, then almost ripped the shirt as I pulled it over my head. The jeans were shoved down my legs before I had kicked off my flats. I just needed that scent away from me.

"Are you okay?" Kai asked from outside the room.

I whirled, arms crossing over my chest, but he wasn't in the doorway and wasn't watching me undress.

The trembling still rattled my body until my teeth chattered. Anger burned my veins and turned my stomach. And then the tears started.

Dropping to the ground with my arms still covering my chest, I hiccupped as a sob wracked my body and tears began to spill over my lashes.

Kai's feet appeared in my vision then disappeared. Then a soft robe was draped over my shoulders and he lowered to the ground until I was between his knees, wrapping himself around my back, his arms hugging me tightly.

A purr rumbled against me, slowly causing the trembles to slow, but the tears continued to flow.

It was a few more minutes before I could find my voice. "Thank you. For stopping him," I said.

His arms simply grew tighter, his purr louder. "You smell like him."

There was a hint of a growl in his words, but he never stopped purring.

Lowering my head, I sniffed. I did still smell like Eric. The tears continued to fall over my lashes as the stress of the night took its toll. I might not have been a typical omega, but my biology, my hormones, my nature still required me to feel safe. And I had not felt safe while Eric had kept me trapped in the bathroom, his hands wandering to places where they weren't granted permission.

"I need a shower," I muttered as I hiccupped again.

Kai stood, scooping me into his arms, and carried me to the bathroom. I wanted to tell him I was fine, that I could shower on my own, that I didn't want him to see me like this.

Instead, I sat on the edge of the tub with the robe wrapped around me and watched as he filled the tub with steaming water and added bubbles and oils and a sparkly bath bomb.

CHAPTER 6

Kai

I hadn't felt the level of rage that I'd felt tonight in years. I had rescued countless omegas through my long career. But never had I felt such a sense of possessiveness, as though that fucker had assaulted my mate. *My* omega.

And she wasn't. Sophie wasn't mine. She was my client. But…

Fuck me.

I would continue to fight the urge to leave my mark on her. I would continue to ignore the need that arose deep inside of me and hardened my cock every time her scent met my nose. Didn't make it any easier, though.

She'd stopped me from beating that Eric fucker to death. Because I had no doubt if I'd started, I wouldn't have stopped raining punches on his face until he was no longer able to move.

Now, she trembled and was doing her best to stop the flow of tears as she huddled in the massive tub in her ensuite bathroom.

I couldn't leave the room. Even when she'd dropped the robe and pushed her underwear to the floor to step into the suds, I couldn't make myself walk through the door. I simply continued to purr, staying close, keeping one hand on her shoulder.

I had never been much help when it came to comforting emotional omegas, but now that was all I wanted. I wanted the fire back in her eyes. I wanted to hear her sass, to hear her insult me.

Better yet, I wanted her to call that fucking pack and tell them they could all go to hell. Then maybe call her parents and tell them the same fucking thing.

Sophie's arms were wrapped around her shins, her cheek resting on her knee. She'd washed off using the stuff she kept in her bathroom but hadn't bothered climbing from the water yet. And I was content staying by her side until she asked for some privacy.

"Thanks again," she muttered so low I'd barely caught it.

I nodded, unable to speak without the growl reentering my voice. She needed me calm. Talking about seeing that asshole hovering over her, reminding me of how fucking petite and fragile she was, would only send a fresh wave of rage simmering through me.

"I didn't...I should have stopped him," she said, only turning her face toward me.

"It looked like you were trying to stop him," I said.

"When he kissed me. I should have stopped him. But I was kind of buzzed. And he smelled good. And I thought..." She sighed, the sound a little shaky. At least the tears had stopped, even if they'd left the tip of her nose pink and her cheeks a little flushed. "My parents are adamant about me packing up. And they acted like they cared...How much bull shit do you think they were feeding me?"

Taking my hand from her shoulder, I turned so I was facing her more directly. "Honestly?"

She dipped her chin in a nod.

"I think it was all bullshit. They waited for you to tell them everything then said exactly what they thought you wanted to hear. They... at least that fucker doesn't appear to be the kind of alpha who would be content with his omega out in the world making her own money instead of at home and accessible at all times. I don't know about the others, but Eric didn't come across as sincere to me. Not from that first dinner."

"What about you?" she asked, her eyes still on my face while she kept her cheek resting on her knees.

"What about me what?"

I lowered onto the floor so we were more eye to eye instead of looming over her.

"Would you let your omega have her own life? Would you let your omega work? Or would you make her stay home, make sure she had dinner on the table when you got home?"

A humorless chuckle left my lips. "For one thing, I don't know what time I'll be home most nights. Anyone willing to put up with my schedule would get tired of making meals that would be ice cold by the time I walked through the door after a mission."

"And the rest?"

"Would I let my omega work? It's not up to me what anyone in my life does. If I ever decided to claim an omega or pack up, her – or his – life would be their own. I would rather someone be a complete person so we could complement each other than have someone revolve their entire existence around being my mate."

She raised her head and watched me, her eyes roaming my face. It was slow, but I watched as her pupils dilated. Then her perfume became heavy and sweet.

I should have left. I should have excused myself. I should have pushed to my feet and gave her my back.

I did none of those things. Not even when she leaned forward, wrapped a hand around my neck, and pulled me closer until our lips touched.

It was gentle at first, merely sipping at each other, our lips molding around each other's. And then her other arm snaked around my neck until her suds covered tits were pressed against my t-shirt covered chest. I didn't give a shit that she was soaking my shirt. I didn't give a shit that my job was to protect her.

My omega needed me. She needed my comfort. She needed what only her alpha could give her.

But I wasn't her alpha.

Standing, I pulled her with me, holding her to my chest as I lifted her from the tub. My tongue was coated in her sweetness, her pheromones hardening my dick until I wondered if the denim of my jeans could restrain it.

Sophie wrapped her legs around my waist, her bare, soaking wet pussy right over the ridge under my jeans. And started to rock her hips.

I was a lost man. Lost in sensation. Lost in her scent.

A whimper escaped her lips and I swallowed it. And then reality slammed into my hindbrain, bringing me back to here and now.

She was officially being courted by a pack. A pack her father had chosen for her. A pack her family approved. And he'd touched her. He'd made her uncomfortable.

Pulling away, I bit back the chuckle when she practically chased my lips.

"Sophie," I said gently, untangling her legs from around my back and gripping her shoulders to put space between us.

I had to keep my eyes on her face and not let them lower to wear beads of water trailed down over her shoulders, over her tits, down her soft belly and down lower…

"Sophie," I barked when she continued to try to climb my body, her hands tugging and pulling at my shirt, my belt, the button of my jeans.

She tensed and stared into my face, her blown pupils slowly bleeding to their pretty, warm brown.

"Why are we stopping?"

Before I lost control, I grabbed the robe she'd laid over the vanity before slipping into the tub and draped it around her shoulders, tugging it closed tightly.

"You…" Fuck. Her chest still heaved with heavy breaths, and her lips were pink and kiss swollen. There was a little irritation around her chin from my beard, and her caramelly sweetness was making me dizzy.

Pushing a hand through my hair, I turned and left the room, hoping to clear my head when I wasn't drowning in her scent.

It took a few minutes, but Sophie joined me in the living room, fully dressed, though her clothes clung to her damp body as though she hadn't bothered fully drying off before tugging on a pair of leggings and a tank top thin enough to showcase her dark pink and hardened nipples.

"What the hell was that all about?" she asked, her anger bright in her eyes as her caramel and floral signature took on a bitter note.

"You're courting a pack, Sophie."

"And one of them tried to rut me in the bathroom during our first date."

"You said you enjoyed his kiss before that."

Her eyes narrowed and she crossed her arms over her chest. "You're not going to be one of those guys who tells me I led him on. No fucking way are you one of those assholes."

"Not at all. But you know how powerful scents can be. Can you honestly tell me you would be even remotely attracted to me if I wore scent blockers?"

I wanted to believe she wanted me, wanted someone like me, but I was in law enforcement. Sure, I was paid well, but nothing like the way she had grown accustomed to in her family. I couldn't spoil her and put her in the kind of palace she deserved the way that pack could. Or any of the packs her father had sent her way so far.

Her brows, a couple shades darker than her pretty blonde hair and perfectly sculpted and arched, slammed together. "You might want to say exactly what you're thinking. Because if I go by the context clues of this conversation, I might end up slapping you again."

Cocking one brow, I said, "You do remember what happened last time. You slap me, I spank you."

The first time, I'd simply wanted to teach her a lesson. I'd had no idea it would have resulted in a hot, albeit short, fuck fest. This time, though, I wondered if I could follow through with it. Especially knowing she was into it. And what would more than likely conspire after.

Perfume didn't explode from her at my words. Instead, her scent turned even more bitter as her eyes narrowed and she waited for me to elaborate.

"You wouldn't want a fucking thing to do with me if you'd met me on the street. You wouldn't have noticed me if we'd seen each other in a bar. You've been locked in a house with me, with an alpha, and your omega is reacting to my scent. Those guys, that pack, can give you the life you want. They have the money to make sure you live in the lap of luxury, that you retain your princess status. And they already offered to finance your future business plans. You really think I have the resources for something like that?"

Now her chest heaved for a different reason. Rage simmered just below the surface as she took slow steps in my direction, her head craning to look up into my face.

"So the only reason I would want a man is because he has money. That's what you're saying. Right?"

I stared down into her face and lifted my shoulders in a shrug.

"Say the words, Kai. I want you to say the fucking words. You still see me as nothing more than a spoiled omega. *Princess*, right?" She said the term with so much venom I swore I felt the force of it like a slap.

Taking a step closer, I forced the growl to stay locked in my chest when her hands clenched into fists. If she hit me, could I bend her over and spank her again?

No. No way. It didn't have the effect I'd planned last time and I was trying to put distance between us and make her understand why I'd stopped us in the bathroom before we'd gone too far.

"You are a spoiled omega who requires a palace. You require attention and gifts and pretty stuff. You *deserve* that. Someone like me…I can't give that to you. I can't buy you a mansion. I can't shower you with gifts and attention when I'm sneaking around outside compounds and shooting at traffickers and rogue alphas. That pack… Eric fucked up." And I still wanted to kill him. "But your father hired me to keep you safe until you found someone to take you in, to bond you. He did not hire me to fuck you or to placate you. He didn't hire me to give you someone to slum with until you found your perfect prince of an alpha."

"Slum," she said, repeating my word. "*Slum?* So you're saying I was whoring around while I wait for someone better." Not a question. And the look in her eye quickly bled from rage…to hurt. I'd hurt her. I'd cut her. I'd hurt her feelings in a way she might never forgive me for.

Tears welled in her eyes. "Fuck you."

She turned and rushed from the room, slamming her bedroom door behind her so hard the windows rattled.

Fuck. I hadn't meant to hurt her. But…

But what? I wanted her. I fucking wanted her so bad it was hard to breathe when I was near her. Which was why I'd kept my distance. I wanted to feel her below my hands, under my body, wrapped around my cock again.

But it was so much more than that. I wanted to know why she'd chosen to go into omega studies, what led her to want to open the facility for omegas. She hadn't mentioned ever being abused; appeared to be extremely sheltered and, yeah, spoiled.

I wanted to know why she was so argumentative, whether any other members of her family were omegas, whether they'd raised her to have such strong opinions or if something had happened to make her push back against any and all possible opposition.

Those were things I would never learn. Not unless we spent more time talking and getting to know each other. And then, I would have to let her go. I would end up falling for her then watch as she packed up with a group of alphas, watch as she was bonded.

I wasn't a masochist. I had no desire to put my heart out there just to have her smash it under her tiny feet.

CHAPTER 7

Sophie

I kept my eyes focused through the windshield as Kai drove me to the pack house a week after Eric had pawed at me and Kai had completely rejected me.

Oh, he hadn't just rejected me. He'd more or less said I was slumming, that I was only interested in him for his dick, that I'd only used him to slake my needs.

Yes, I was pulled in by his scent. Yes, his warm cookie and woodsy scent did yummy things to my body. But it was so much more than that. He was strong. He was attractive. And he protected omegas for a living. He literally risked his life to protect those like me.

Maybe I didn't know nearly enough about him to say I was developing deep feelings for him, but there was something about him that tugged at my heart and made me wonder about my future, about how a future with him would look.

He either didn't see me in the same light or truly thought I believed I was too good for him. So stupid.

Instead of doing what I really wanted and screaming at him, fighting him, making him listen to me, making him understand I wasn't like my family, that I didn't care about wealth or status, I sat like the good little spoiled omega in an expensive dress my father had had delivered as my personal security delivered me to my prospective pack.

I'd yet to meet the pack of eight. My fathers saw it as a good sign that I was willing to court this pack. Even after I'd explained to Daddy Jim what had happened with Eric, he'd blown it off, explaining that alphas knew what they wanted and often had a hard time controlling their baser urges when they found their omega.

Bullshit. Eric was horny. I was unbonded and available. It might have been biology, but that didn't mean he'd had the right to try to force himself on me.

Being as the thought of trying to force any kind of relationship with eight alphas made me queasy and anxious, I decided to give this pack, including Eric, one more chance.

Eric had called and apologized profusely. He'd had flowers sent to the house almost every day until I agreed to give them another shot.

And Kai was back to avoiding me at all costs, merely becoming a ghost in the house. I only knew he still lived there by the baked sweetness that permeated any room he vacated when he heard my approach.

Even now, the only sound that filled the cab of his SUV was the music coming from the speakers. He'd used scent blocking soap before we'd left. I could barely get a hint of his warmth through the chemically altered spicy smell of the bodywash.

I'd contemplated doing the same since Eric had made it sound as though my scent was what had driven him to his near rut. But we needed to know if we were compatible, and a large part of that was based on our signatures.

Only Chris stood on the stoop when Kai parked. I glanced at my guard and chauffeur in time to catch a frown before he smoothed the wrinkle between his brows and returned his face to a neutral expression.

Chris made it to my door and offered a hand before Kai could round the hood. He didn't look at me, didn't growl, simply shadowed us up the stairs and into the house, then took up sentry across the room where he leaned against the wall with his hands crossed in front of him and his eyes straight ahead.

I hated this. I hated this distance. I almost preferred the heated arguments. I missed the few days we'd had when we were attempting to get to know each other.

I missed thinking there was some kind of possibility of a life with someone like Kai.

"You look beautiful," Chris said, lifting my hand to his lips where he feathered a soft kiss across the back.

"Thank you," I said, dipping my head.

Maybe it was time I behaved accordingly. Maybe it was time to be who Kai thought I was, how he saw me. Maybe it was time to allow four princes to dote on their princess, to spoil their omega. Fuck the dreams I'd had for my future. Apparently, all anyone saw when they discovered my designation was a womb, a toy, a prize.

And perhaps that was all there was to me. How had I truly believed I could make a difference when even someone like Kai, someone strong, someone who had no problem putting me in my place with a slap across my ass saw me as nothing more than a spoiled rotten omega?

My heart ached, but I pushed it away, pushed it down deep, and kept my chin raised. I thought of my mom, of my sister, my brother. They lived in the lap of luxury. They didn't work. They sat at home while their alphas provided them with anything and everything their heart desired.

That wasn't what I wanted for my life. But…apparently, there was nothing I could do about that. It was time to accept my fate.

Chris escorted me into the house, and I frowned up at him when I didn't spot any of the others.

"We decided it might be easier to court you one at a time. Let you get to know us individually instead of bombarding you from every direction."

Without the distraction of the others, Chris's warm coffee scent wrapped around me like a blanket. It didn't stir my omega, didn't cause slick to dampen my panties or thighs, but it was pleasant enough.

"Since dinner didn't go so well last time, I had our staff make dessert, instead. Unless you're hungry. I can have them make something more substantial."

I smiled politely, lowering my eyes demurely. Good omega. Submissive. That was how they wanted me.

Bile rose in my throat, and I caught myself glancing in Kai's direction. It was as though he was more turned on any time we argued or bickered.

But I wasn't here to impress Kai. I was here under orders of my family to find and secure a pack who would ensure my future was safe. To ensure I would carry on the family line.

Both my siblings had given birth to alphas and omegas, only one beta in the mix. And I knew my parents hoped for the same from me. As though I had a say in the matter. As though I could will my ovaries into creating any specific designation.

"Dessert sounds perfect," I said with a forced smile.

Could Chris see through it? Could he tell how tense I was, how hard I was struggling to keep up the façade?

The dress my father had chosen and sent to the house hugged my body like the first I'd worn to dinner with this pack. It dipped lower, though, showing more cleavage. I'd donned another pair of heels and made sure to wear the diamond studs I'd been gifted the day I had presented as an omega, as though merely existing was enough to earn such an expensive gift.

The table was long, the leaves that had been removed the first time I was here had been reinserted. Chris sat me in a chair to the right of the head, then took his seat. We waited for the staff to carry in plates and silverware, then set a beautiful cheesecake drizzled with strawberry sauce and slices before us.

Chris didn't make a move to serve me; simply watched me as his hired people sliced a piece and set it on my plate first, then his.

"Dessert wine, madam?" the woman asked. Beta, if her clean, fruity scent was anything to go by.

"Yes. Thank you," I replied with a polite dip of my head.

I might hate this kind of life, might have hoped to escape it once I became an adult, but I had been trained well by my domineering alpha fathers.

Unfolding the cloth napkin, I shook it out and placed it over my lap, thanking the beta once more when she poured my glass of wine, then Chris's.

"To second chances," he said, raising his glass.

Tears burned the backs of my eyes, but I blinked and forced another smile. "To second chances," I repeated, waiting until he barely touched his glass to mine.

The wine was delicious. The dessert was decadent and rich and pure perfection. These aspects of the life I'd known growing up were welcome. They were amazing.

The rest?

Either I had to accept my destiny, accept I was no one and could never do a damn thing to change anyone's opinions of my designation, or I ended up defying my family.

And then I would be literally out on my ass. I hadn't been allowed to find a job after college. I had my degree, but that would only come in handy if the Omega Center was hiring, and it wasn't necessary to teach omegas what to expect during their first heats or teaching alphas how to care for their omegas.

The latter seemed as though it should be second nature. How hard was it to be gentle and kind to someone you loved, someone who was obviously going through something painful?

"Join me in the living room? Unless you'd like another slice," Chris said.

He was sweet. He was polite. But there was no strong reaction from my omega.

"I would love another glass of wine," I said.

He stood and pulled out my chair for me, grabbed the bottle of wine by the neck, then offered his elbow. "We'll take the whole thing with us. It's just the two of us. Uh…three of us. I apologize. Kai, would you like a slice of cheesecake? Or a glass of wine?"

"No, sir. Thank you, sir."

My nose curled at Kai's response. I knew it was his training coming through, but it felt as though he was another member of Chris's hired staff. I liked it better when he was gruff, when he glared and growled.

He silently followed us from the dining room and into the large sitting room. If there was a television set here, it was hidden. There was a large U-shaped couch that would fit the whole pack, and a stone fireplace that crackled, the fire warming the air.

"Please. Have a seat," he said, taking my glass and refilling it before setting the bottle on a table and taking his seat beside me.

We chatted and talked. He asked me more questions about my business plan. Kai's words came roaring back in my head.

"Can we be honest with each other?" I said, setting my glass down as my thoughts became fuzzy with a slight buzz. If I drank much more, I would end up saying exactly what I thought and how I felt. And according to Daddy Jim, he was running out of favors to call in for profitable and successful packs to mate with his remaining unbonded daughter.

"I would prefer that." Chris did as I had and set his wine on the table beside mine.

"The four of you – you don't want an omega who works full time. You're looking for an omega to carry pups, to carry on your name."

His eyes hardened a second before they dropped to where he took my hand into his. "I meant what I said about supporting your plans to build something to help omegas. But we…I would prefer my mate to be at home. I would prefer my omega to be receptive to motherhood. Your father told us of your desperate situation. I believe we can give you the life you're used to. If you'd like to help build this…organization, we will support you. We will even fund it. But we would prefer you remain as an advisor and stay behind the scenes."

I nodded my head as another wave of emotion clogged my throat. Kai had seen right through their bull shit.

And Chris had just reminded me of my desperate situation. An unbonded twenty-eight-year-old omega. Alone in the world. If my fathers cut me off, I would be in danger of any alpha who decided they wanted to claim me, to bond me, to force a permanent union.

My choices had been all but taken away within a few weeks. How had I thought my life would be any different? How had I believed I could make a difference?

How had I been so naïve as to believe I had any say in my future?

Chris turned to look over his shoulder at Kai. "Has her father given permission to be left alone with us?"

"I'm not to leave the house," Kai said, his eyes straight ahead. I didn't miss the way his jaw was tight, the twitch in his cheek, the way he held his shoulders.

"But you could leave the room?"

Kai turned his eyes to me as though asking my permission. Or maybe asking whether I was comfortable being alone with Chris.

What fucking choice did I have? It was between his pack or a group of eight alphas. Or worse – alone in a world that wasn't meant for omegas.

Dipping my head, I tried to keep the fear and sorrow from my face when he searched it. I knew he could see through it, see through the watery smile I gave him even as I tried to steel myself for whatever would come the moment Kai left the room.

"I'll be in the kitchen," Kai said, his eyes on me.

I knew all I would have to do was call out and he would rush back in. Because he was paid to protect me.

Because he cared about me.

I knew he did. He didn't need to say the words. He'd protected me from Eric. He'd purred for me, helped me into a bath, helped me calm down, and then kissed me until I was barely able to think straight. Or I had kissed him.

Either way, he could hide it all he wanted, he could fight against it all he wanted. He wanted me. He cared for me.

And the two of us could never have anything past client and body-guard. Because I was nothing more than an omega.

"Your father hired a good man," Chris said once Kai left the room.

I nodded, swallowing hard when Chris's hand took mine and his thumb stroked soft circles across the back.

"We want to give you a good life, little omega. We want to spoil you. Give you anything you could ever want." He waved around the room. "We can build on another wing if you're willing to give us more than one pup. I know each of us would love to attempt to give you one from each of us."

He leaned forward and pressed a tender kiss to my lips. It was soft and sweet. Not demanding like Eric's. Not toe curling like Kai's.

Under the rich coffee scent was something spicy, like cardamom or cinnamon. Delicious, but I didn't feel the need to press my nose to his throat and drown in it.

Chris pulled back and pressed a hand to my cheek. "Since we are officially courting you, I need to ask an…uncomfortable question."

I knew what it was before he voiced it. The same question each pack had already asked.

"Have you had a cycle recently? And would you want us to help you through the next heat, or would you prefer we have things delivered to help you through while we're still getting to know each other."

Would I prefer their knots or a bunch of sex toys?

Yep. He was right. This was a very uncomfortable conversation.

I fought the urge to look for Kai. I half-anticipated the growl he'd released each time the others had asked about my heat.

But he was doing as he was hired and keeping his distance. He was letting the princess be courted by one of four princes.

"I…" I cleared my throat, grabbed the wine glass and downed the last of the contents, wincing a little at the burn in my throat. "I'll let you know what I decide when the time comes."

His nostrils flared and he leaned forward. "I apologize for Eric's behavior, but he got one thing right – you smell amazing." He nuzzled my throat, his tongue barely touching the skin at my pulse point.

I might not have been as affected by Chris as I was by Kai, but between the alcohol and my fucking hormones, the mere touch forced my perfume from me in a heady cloud.

A purr rattled forth from Chris's chest. He gripped my hips and pulled me closer until I would either fall into his lap or had to lift a leg to straddle his thighs.

My dress hitched up, revealing the lacy panties I'd worn beneath. Chris wasn't the man I wanted below me. His hands weren't the ones I wanted smoothing down my sides and up my back as he kissed and nibbled at my throat and shoulder.

But I had to be a good omega. This man would soon be my alpha. I would have no choice but to attend to his desires and one day, spread my legs and accept his seed, to carry his pup. To carry a pup for each of them.

How the hell did they think they could plan that? Would they simply take turns during each cycle in hopes of being the one who fertilized my eggs?

Chris's hands smoothed down my back and cupped my ass, pulling me closer until my underwear covered core was directly over his hard length.

He slanted his mouth over mine, his tongue teasing the seam until I opened for him. He moaned into my mouth when I placed my hands on his shoulders, keeping myself steady as he set a rhythm, using my body to bring us both pleasure.

My biology took over under the control of an alpha and the tingles of release built as slick coated my panties, no doubt seeping through to cover his slacks.

If he noticed, he didn't appear to mind.

"Your body is so reactive. Such a good little omega," he purred against my lips.

A good little omega. Good little omega. That was my role. It was my job to please my alpha.

I had fought against it for so long, but my future was right here in this ridiculously large house with an alpha using my body to get himself off. He was rocking his hips against me, his knot evident and swollen through the material of his pants as it pressed against my clit.

Whether I wanted to or not, my body was receptive to his alpha hormones. My fingers dug into his shoulders as he kissed me again, a licking, wet, messy kiss as his hips moved faster, as he tugged me faster, until my pussy clenched and spilled my release.

I bit back the moan, refusing to voice the pleasure he'd given me, ashamed to allow Kai to hear what we were doing while he waited in the kitchen, refusing to acknowledge that he was right. My life was planned, and nothing he or I did could change that.

Chris buried his face in my throat and grunted as he came in his pants, his hips jerking a few times before he relaxed, his breath warming my chest.

"Such a beautiful little omega. So perfect for me. So perfect for us."

CHAPTER 8

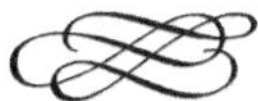

Kai

Pheromones lifted on the air as I stood in the kitchen, pacing silently and waiting for any word from Sophie that she needed me.

When I was finally beckoned to the foyer, she wouldn't look at me. But I could smell her release. And I could smell *his* release. There was no way they'd fucked, not without making any sounds, not with paid staff walking around the house or with me in the other room.

But they'd both found release in some way. And she didn't have that same glow I'd seen on her face the one and only time I'd felt her fall apart around me.

In fact, she looked…ashamed. Or maybe embarrassed. Chris didn't seem to notice as he twined his fingers through hers and escorted her out to my SUV, then bent to take her lips in a long, deep goodbye kiss.

"I can't wait to see you again," he said, pressing one more quick kiss to her lips. "I believe Anton is dying to see you next. Don't be surprised if you hear from him before the sun's up. I thought he was going to beat Eric to a pulp for almost ruining everything with you."

Asshole. Or maybe he wasn't. He wasn't saying anything rude, wasn't doing anything that made Sophie pull away or push at his chest. But…

But what? The only reason he was an asshole was because I was jealous. That was it. He was saying and doing things I wanted to do with Sophie. He could give her the life she deserved while I would do nothing but break her heart or leave her a widow.

"I'm looking forward to it," she said, lowering her head and looking up at him through her lashes.

Who the hell was this woman? This wasn't the omega who'd told visiting packs how she felt about them, the woman who'd teased a pack and told them she planned to court several at one time. This wasn't the woman who'd stood toe to toe with me, argued her case, demanded I be honest with her.

This wasn't the omega who'd sassed me, who'd slapped me, who'd been turned on by a spanking and had jumped my bones.

This woman…this was a stereotypical omega. She looked…Sophie looked as though her spirit had been broken.

I had heard her soft voice through her bedroom door when she'd told her dad of the events that had unfolded the night Eric had tried to rut her in the fucking bathroom. I'd heard the defeat in her voice as she'd finally relented and agreed to give the pack another shot.

And I could see the defeat in her eyes now as she forced a smile up at Chris and accepted another kiss before he opened the door and waited until she was settled in her seat.

The cab wreaked of alpha. And her normally sweet, sticky scent was bitter, like burned sugar and something else, something cloying.

The temptation to pull the SUV over, drag her into my arms, and purr for her was nearly overwhelming. But I'd already decided to give her the space she would need to find her pack, to form a family. It wasn't my job to comfort her. I wasn't her alpha. She wasn't my omega.

Reaching forward, I turned the knob on the radio, increasing the volume of the music in hopes of drowning out my own thoughts. It did nothing for the heady stench in the vehicle.

I hated this. I hated the way she smelled covered in another alpha's signature. Hated the bitter tang of whatever was upsetting her.

She hadn't called out to me for help. And I could smell her release. She'd orgasmed. So why did she seem so upset now? Why did she look so tense sitting beside me as though she were holding back tears?

The moment I put the SUV in park, she pushed from her seat and nearly sprinted up the stairs, then waited with her arms crossed over her chest until I unlocked and pushed the door open.

A sniffle clenched my heart as she made a beeline for her bedroom, closing the door and shutting me out. The pipes squeaked as she turned on the shower. She'd come with Chris and was ready to wash his scent from her body.

Didn't omegas relish in being covered by their alpha's essence? Shouldn't she have been happy that she'd found a pack?

Of course she wasn't. I'd barely recognized the woman tonight, barely recognized her face as her warm eyes had turned hard and emotionless.

I wasn't sure how long I stood there staring at her closed door. There was still an overwhelming urge to rush into her room, to take her into my arms, to chase away whatever the hell had made her retreat into herself.

But I didn't.

Entering my own room, I kicked off my shoes, pulled my shirt off, and kicked my pants down my legs. I had no desire to hang out in the living room in case she wasn't quite ready for bed. I wasn't sure I could see that look in her eyes and keep my hands to myself.

And I sure as fuck didn't want to detect even the slightest hint of that alpha's signature on her skin.

Dropping onto my bed, I sat on the edge, resting my elbows on my knees and putting my face in my hands.

I wanted a different life. I had never begrudged my designation, had never wished I was anything but a soldier for the ORE. I loved that I made a difference.

But since meeting Sophie, something had begun to shift inside of me. If I'd been born in a different family, if I'd chosen a different line of work, I might have been an acceptable choice for her family. I might have been given the blessing to court her instead of standing by while other men enjoyed her time, while other men tried to earn her respect, her heart.

I wasn't sure how long I sat there feeling sorry for myself. But when the knob on my door squeaked softly as it turned, I jerked my head up and watched with a deep furrow of my brows as Sophie stepped into my room completely naked, beads of water trailing down her body, her hair sopping wet and hanging in thick tendrils over her shoulders and teasing the tips of her nipples.

She crossed the room, that same devoid look in her eyes, and dropped to her knees between my thighs.

"Sophie–" I started, reaching for her, but she batted my hands away.

Her fingers shook as she pulled the front of my boxers away and released my already hard cock, the knot at the base swelling and throbbing at the sight of her on her knees before me.

She didn't look at me, didn't raise her eyes to my face as she circled her thin, cool fingers around my girth and gave it a slow tug. And then she lowered her mouth and took me into her throat.

"Fuck. Sophie–" But I couldn't get anything else out as she began to bob on my length, one of her hands cupping my sac, the other squeezing my knot until my muscles tensed, my balls tightened, and I came hard.

She pulled back, lifting so that my spurts hit her tits, her chest, and her throat. Releasing me, she lifted one hand and rubbed my cum into her skin as though coating herself in my scent.

Then she stood, turned, and left me staring after her as she pulled the door closed behind her, her own door closing seconds later.

What the fuck had just happened?

Sophie

. . .

I DIDN'T BOTHER DRESSING after leaving Kai's room. And part of me wished I'd been wearing something when I'd covered myself in his cum. Then, I could roll in it every night instead of having to wash his scent from me before each date with the guys from the pack.

Just because I'd resigned myself to fall into the role of dutiful little omega didn't mean I couldn't have a few secrets. It didn't mean I couldn't have my little guilty pleasures. And, like Kai had said, I enjoyed slumming with him.

What an ugly word. Being with him, tasting him, feeling him didn't feel like slumming. It felt normal, natural. He felt like home. He felt like he was the missing part of my heart, of my soul.

Being with Chris had felt...forced. I'd felt as though I was merely a puppet, like the night had been choreographed and I'd played my part to perfection.

But this, what I'd done with Kai, the sticky warm cookie scent drying on my skin, felt like it was just for me. Like I'd made him a part of me, like I could carry him with me forever even after I left this house, after I moved into the pack house with Bryan, Chris, Anton, and Eric.

Curling my knees to my chest, I wrapped my arms around my shins and stared at the dark room inside my walk-in closet. The omega in me wanted that nest. She wanted to crawl inside and wrap up in every single blanket present.

But I wouldn't taint the space. It was too precious. And even after my shower, even after scrubbing at my skin, even after coating my skin with Kai's release, I could still detect hints of Chris on my flesh, on my body.

I supposed I should get used to it. And maybe I should do what was needed to purge any and all desire for Kai from my heart and mind. When I was younger, I thought sleeping with a crush would help get over the want. But being with Kai again would do nothing but further my feelings and need for him in my life.

Our time together was temporary. And then he would go off to save another life. He would be assigned to protect another unbonded omega.

And maybe he'd fuck her, too.

Kai

Sitting on the back porch with a mug of coffee in my hand, I watched as Sophie passed through the kitchen. Her hair was already set in perfect waves. Her face was fresh with makeup. She wore a pair of jeans that hugged her ass beautifully, a blouse that hung off her freckle kissed shoulders while revealing a deep dip in the back to reveal the flawless skin of her back.

My gaze roamed down to her feet where they were encased in a pair of high heeled boots. It was barely seven in the morning. Did she have plans with one of the alphas?

One of *her* alphas. It was all but set in stone. She was courting them. They would take turns bringing her gifts, bringing her pleasure. All while I waited in another room.

At what point would her father find it acceptable for her to be left alone with that pack? Was he old-fashioned and would make them all wait until a bonding ceremony? Would she be forced to wait until one or all of the alphas left their claiming marks on her beautifully soft skin?

Or would her family simply rejoice that they'd finally been able to tie her to a wealthy pack and give their blessings within days of their courtship?

As she turned, a mug between her hands, her eyes caught on me and she stopped, simply studying me a few seconds before giving me her back and sitting at the kitchen table.

A hundred things flew through my mind, so many things I wanted to say to her, but I kept my ass parked in the chair on the patio. If she had plans, if I was to escort her somewhere, she would let me know and I would be ready to go when it was time.

For now, I would give her space. If she wanted to talk to me, she could step outside. Although those pointy ass heels might get caught in the spaces between the wood boards of the deck.

After a while, the little bit of coffee left in my mug grew cold. I would either have to continue sitting here or go inside to top it off. I hadn't quite had enough caffeine yet, especially if I was going to be chauffeuring her to play with her new pack.

The door opened silently and I stepped through, hoping to stay as far under the radar as possible. I knew she would be aware of my presence from scent alone but wanted to get in and out as quickly as possible.

"I'm sorry about last night," she said without turning to look at me. "I had no right."

If she wanted me to tell her she hadn't been welcome in my room last night, that I hadn't loved every second of her hands and mouth on me, she'd be waiting a long fucking time.

Topping off my coffee, I turned and headed back for the porch.

"You were right about them," she said softly.

"About what?"

Her shoulders rose and fell, and I could have sworn I heard the softest sigh at the sound of my voice.

Sophie turned in her chair and looked up into my face. "Everything they'd said was bullshit. They aren't supportive of my plans for my future. It was all...it was bullshit."

"I know."

She blinked rapidly as though fighting tears and darted her attention away from me. "My parents have chosen this pack. No," she said with a mirthless laugh. "My *fathers* have chosen this pack. I'm to do everything in my power to make sure they choose me back. I'm to do as asked, to make the pack want to claim me."

My stomach turned and red began to tint the edges of my vision as rage burned through my veins. "What the fuck does that mean?"

Only her eyes turned to me. "I'm an omega, Kai. I have one job.

You were right. I'm nothing more than a princess and I belong in a gilded cage. My life was planned for me the day I presented. Nothing I've done…nothing I'll ever do will change that."

She shrugged her narrow shoulders, pushed to her feet, and emptied the last of her coffee into the sink.

And I was left watching her and feeling as though someone had punched me in the stomach, the throat, and the nuts all at once.

I hated myself for the shit I'd said to her. I'd lashed out for no other reason than jealousy. Maybe some of it was jealousy of the way she'd grown up, for the way her designation was coddled and cared for.

But the biggest part – even if I wasn't aware at the time – was that I would never be good enough for someone like her. And jealousy over the alphas that would have her in their lives forever.

CHAPTER 9

Sophie

Anton and I sat cuddled on the couch watching some historical romance. I wasn't sure whether that was his preferred genre or if he was trying to seduce me with the sexy scenes.

Of the four, his scent was probably the most enticing. Warm and cozy, like old books from the library. It didn't hurt that he had the same inky black hair and the same crystalline blue eyes as Kai. And, yeah, I was comparing the two, trying to find the same desire for this alpha that I felt for the man who was currently leaning against the wall at our backs.

Anton had offered him a drink, offered him a meal, had even offered to let him sit on the couch.

But Kai refused. Simply stood there, his shoulders pressed against the wall, his hands clasped in front of him, his eyes glued to the TV show as though he could pretend Anton and I didn't exist.

Anton's arm tightened around my shoulders, and he tugged me

closer until my cheek rested against his shoulder, my knees on the couch and bent toward him, pressing against his thigh.

Reaching behind us, Anton grabbed a blanket and draped it over my bare legs. Of course, I was wearing yet another dress for a one-on-one date. Because my job was to make these alphas want me. To make them believe I wanted them. To be desirable and agreeable and pleasing to their every sense.

A soft purr rumbled from Anton, vibrating against my ear as I nuzzled my cheek closer, resting a hand on his firm chest. A chest, I noted, that wasn't nearly as broad or muscular as Kai's.

Damn it. How was I supposed to push him out of my mind and focus on the men I was supposed to be courting if he was always around, his scent always surrounding me like a blanket, if I was always aware of his every glance in my direction?

I would have to ask permission from my fathers for some alone time with my soon-to-be alphas. I had a feeling they would still require an escort, but maybe they would give permission for Kai to wait in the SUV while each of these alphas did their best to seduce me and entice me into joining their pack and becoming their omega.

"I got you something," Anton whispered into my ear, his breath sending shivers through my body.

Lifting my head, I smiled sweetly. "You did?" My voice sounded sickeningly sweet even in my own ears.

Good little omega.

He reached into his pocket and pulled out a velvet box, holding it in his palm and waiting for me to take it.

Pushing up a little, I took the box and popped the lid back, staring down at the sapphire earrings sparkling back at me. "Oh my gosh," I breathed.

Okay. I really didn't need expensive gifts. I was never the kind of woman who was won over by presents, but by actions.

But these were beautiful.

"I wanted you to have something that would make you think of me every time you wore them."

As I looked into his face, I realized the earrings were the same color as his eyes.

"Thank you. They're absolutely beautiful."

Anton's smile was genuine as he leaned forward slowly, giving me time and space to decide whether I wanted to close the distance and accept his kiss. I did everything in my power to forget Kai was in the room as I slanted my mouth over his, humming in approval when he gently cupped my cheek, sipping and nipping at my lips.

It wasn't exactly uncommon for packs like this to have hired staff or for said staff to walk in on some unfortunate and embarrassing times. Embarrassing for the staff. The alphas rarely noticed anything outside of where their dick was currently buried.

The box was removed from my hand, and then I was being urged backward until I was lying stretched on the couch, Anton settling between my thighs. I was vaguely aware of the sound of heavy thuds of boots retreating as Anton smoothed a hand down my side and buried the other in my hair, tilting my head to deepen the kiss.

If this had been a normal date, I would have worn pants in case this very scenario played out. Instead, my skirt had hiked up, like it had with Chris, and Anton's hard length was pressed against my core, the throbbing swell of his knot pressed against my clit.

"You smell so sweet," Anton said against my lips, his hips making slow movements.

I squeezed my eyes shut as his hand smoothed up to cup one of my breasts through my dress, squeezing a nipple through the material. It felt amazing. But it wasn't the hand I wanted on me. This wasn't the man I wanted between my thighs.

And it wasn't the fingers I wanted pushing past the elastic of my panties to explore my slicked folds. My body was reacting to Anton more than it had the others. But at no point did I feel the mindless need I had with Kai. At no point did I feel the need to be covered in his cum, to be covered in his essence, in his scent.

"Sweet little omega," Anton whispered in my ear as he nuzzled and nipped at the sensitive skin there, lapping at my pulse point.

My breath caught in my lungs when I felt the drag of his teeth along the place where my neck met my shoulder. Not yet. I knew that was exactly what my family wanted. I knew they would be overjoyed to learn one of the alphas had been so overcome by me that they'd marked me, bonded me, made me their omega.

But I wanted to pretend I still had some visage of freedom, at least for a few more days. Or weeks.

He didn't bite. But he did suck on that spot, lick it, nip at it as his fingers toyed with my sex, stroking my clit, sliding into my pussy to stroke that most sensitive spot.

"Such a good little omega. I can feel your cunt clenching my fingers already."

Good little omega.

I should have preened at the praise. I should have swelled with pride that this alpha was pleased by me.

All I felt was dismay. Each time one of these men praised me, I felt as though another nail had been hammered into my coffin, as though my life was being forged by their words.

His hips kept pumping, his hard length pressed against my thigh as he worked his fingers into my pussy, the wet sounds of my slick filling the air. He grunted as he came inside his pants, wetting my thigh through his slacks, a second before my body tightened and I exploded, clenching his fingers until my release trailed between my ass cheeks and onto the back of my dress and the expensive leather couch.

"Holy hell," he breathed as though he'd pumped into me, as though we'd fucked.

Slowly and gently, he pulled his fingers from me and licked them clean, his eyes on me, a soft smile on the corners of his lips.

"I can't wait to feel you clenched around my dick. I bet my good little omega can take a knot like a champ."

Good little omega.

I couldn't find the energy to force a smile, just tilted my chin up when he lowered his face to take my mouth in another licking, deep, wet kiss.

Anton helped clean me up, gently wiping the slick and release from me with a warm, wet washcloth. When it was time to go, he'd had to hunt Kai down, finding him standing on the front stoop, his thick arms crossed over his chest.

Kai nodded at Anton, then walked behind us as I was escorted to the SUV, helped inside, then buckled in place like a child.

In such a short time, I'd gone from believing I could change the world – or at least *my* world – to behaving the way that was expected of me. From the moment my fathers had blown off the fact Eric hadn't taken no for an answer and had had to be pulled off me by the security they'd hired, the fight had all but been beaten from me.

Silence filled the cab just like last time. At least this time, I didn't race for the shower to wash away Anton's scent. But I did bathe the second I was behind my closed bedroom door.

My life was spiraling out of my control and there was only one stable thing in my life that felt as if I could grab onto to keep from disappearing completely.

I didn't bother to dress. I didn't bother to question the wisdom. Simply dried off and made my way across the hall and let myself into Kai's bedroom without knocking.

He was on his back, an arm under his head as he stared at the ceiling. But his boxers were tented, no doubt from the perfume that clung to my skin from my orgasm.

When his head rolled to look at me, a frown was etched deeply between his brows.

But he didn't speak. Didn't ask what I was doing. Didn't ask what I wanted.

Crossing the room, I grabbed the hem of his boxers and dragged them down his legs, staring him in the eye the entire time, waiting for him to stop me, waiting for him to protest, waiting for him to remind me I had a pack of alphas who were days away from claiming me.

The mattress dipped below me as I climbed beside him, lifting a leg to straddle his hips, then gripped him and stroked the blunt head of his cock along my opening, mixing the drop of precum at his slit with my slick.

I lowered onto him with ease, giving myself only a few seconds to adjust to his body before I was rising and falling on him, taking him as deeply as I could without pushing onto his knot.

This was what I needed. This was one of the first moments since I'd been delivered to this house that I felt like myself, that I felt as though my life was my own. The only other two times...were with Kai. The first time we'd fucked on the couch, then when I'd sucked him off and covered myself in his release.

Kai's hands were warm as they gripped my hips and helped raise me then shove me down, increasing the speed, increasing the pressure.

"Tell me what you need, Sophie."

"I need..." *My life. My freedom.*

You.

He sat up, hugging me tightly to him, before flipping me onto my back and plunging into me. He hooked one of my knees over his elbow, opening me further.

"Tell me," he growled, his thrusts so hard his balls were slapping against my ass.

More. I needed more. I needed his knot. I needed him.

I needed his *bite.*

Turning my head to the side, I whimpered. "Please. Bite. Make me yours."

A growl so loud it rumbled the bed exploded from him. The bed rocked and shook below us as his thrusts became frantic and desperate. He dipped his head, his lips latching over my shoulder, his teeth grazing the skin.

"Yes. Please."

In one hard push, he slammed his cock forward until his knot stretched my pussy then entered, rubbing every single pleasure point inside of me.

Crying out, I dragged my nails down his back, shoving my shoulder into his mouth in hopes of puncturing my flesh on his teeth.

Kai rutted inside me as we stayed locked together, his warm jets of cum filling me until our release spilled out and pooled below me onto his bed.

After a few minutes, the aftershocks began to fade to slight tingles and Kai's thrusting hips slowed to a stop. He held his weight from me on his elbows, his face buried in my neck, his breath warming the skin there.

"I can never bite you, Sophie. You're not mine," he said against my skin, the sound slightly muffled. "But I'll give you every part of me you need until your pack officially claims you."

His arms wrapped around my back and hugged me to him.

And that was when the tears welled and spilled over. There wasn't a thing I could do to stop them as I whimpered and clung to him, my last lifeline before my life was gifted to four alphas my heart didn't recognize.

Kai

I HADN'T TRULY UNDERSTOOD why she'd blown me that night. Hadn't understood why she'd covered her tits in my release.

Then tonight, I'd had to leave the room when it was obvious Sophie and Anton were going to fool around. They needed their privacy. She didn't need me hovering around, being a perv and watching her fall apart for another man.

After tonight, I understood. She'd taken my words to heart. She'd taken her fathers' words to heart.

Good little omega. That was all that was expected of her. That was all she was to this world.

But not to me.

She knew there could never be anything between us. And even though I'd thrown the same fucking words in her face, I was safe. I was her comfort. She could be herself around me. She didn't have to plaster on that fake smile or curl her hair or wear those ridiculous shoes around me.

So, I would sacrifice whatever was left of me to Sophie until our last minute together. I would let her take anything and everything from me until her alphas claimed her and moved her into their home.

What I could never give her was my bite. I shouldn't have given her my knot. I assumed she was on birth control because of the way she spoke of helping other omegas. And she wasn't in heat, so the odds of her getting pregnant tonight were slim to none.

Little by little, I would tear little pieces from myself to keep her together until I no longer had anything left to give.

I owed her an apology. A big one. I'd said the words but that was not how I saw her. I had lashed out to protect my own heart every time I felt as though I was growing too attached. And I'd been one of the fuckers who'd helped to start the splintering of her heart, of her spirit.

Rolling us to our sides, my knot still locked inside of her, I threaded my fingers through her hair and pressed my lips to the tip of her nose, her forehead, each cheek, kissing the tears away that continued to roll down her temples to soak into her hair and the pillow below.

Families like hers wouldn't accept the fact she didn't want the life they'd laid out for her. The day one of her dads had called, insisting she continue courting the pack even after Eric had touched her against her will, she'd left her room with slumped shoulders and tear swollen eyes.

"They'll disown you if you walk away from this pack," I said rather than asked.

She nodded, her hair tickling my chin.

"Is there no one else? No other family? What about the Omega Center?"

She had planned to build a network to help omegas who were in the same situation she was currently in, to help them build a life, find a job, protect themselves.

When she shook her head, I lifted a hand to capture her face and tilt her head to look into my eyes, a sentiment right on my tongue.

I'll take care of you. You can stay with me.

But those words stayed frozen in my throat. My life wasn't safe for someone like Sophie. I knew other members of ORE who had omegas, but they were packs. There were multiple members who could take turns watching over their most precious family member.

It was just me. Meaning she would be alone any time I went to work. She would face unknown enemies who might discover where I lived. And I sure as fuck didn't make enough money to buy her sapphire fucking earrings or a house big enough to house an entire football team.

"You can have any part of me until it's time for you to go. But I can never bite you. You know that, right? I won't be the cause for you to lose your family. I won't be the reason they turn their backs on you. I'm not...you need alphas like Anton, or Chris. Men who can make sure you're safe and taken care of."

"You're not good enough," she whispered.

"What?"

"You were going to say you're not good enough."

I was. But I'd stopped myself for both of our sakes.

"I'm...no. I'm not."

She snorted a soft sound and wiggled, testing my knot. When she was able, she pulled away from me, but didn't leave the bed. I would have to change the sheets.

Or maybe I would keep them on a little longer so I could wallow in her scent even after she'd moved in with her new pack.

CHAPTER 10

Sophie

"I'm just feeling a little under the weather," I lied to one of my dads. It was Daddy Michael this time. He was the easiest one to speak to and the least likely to demand I continue courting the pack if I was sick.

"Is it your heat?" he asked.

"No," I said a little too quickly. "No. I'm just a little tired. And my stomach's upset. I wouldn't want to show up and give the pack some kind of stomach virus," I lied.

"Anton said the two of you really connected last night," he said with a soft chuckle, and I hoped that didn't mean the alpha had given my family details of the night's events.

"Yeah. He's nice," I said, trying to sound enthusiastic. "Would you mind giving him or one of the others a call? Tell them I need a few days. Maybe a week. I look terrible. Got to look my best, right?" I smiled in hopes of Michael hearing it over the line but worried it sounded as though I was speaking through clenched teeth.

"I'll give them a call. You rest. Do you need us to send anything? Soup? Heating pad?"

"I'm fine. I'll send my security if I need something that isn't here. Thank you, Daddy Michael."

We ended the call and I sighed in relief.

Kai's words bounced around in my head as I stared down at the dark phone. In the time we'd spent together, last night was the first time I'd seen a warmer, softer side of him.

You can have any part of me until it's time for you to go.

But I *would* have to go. I was going to do everything in my power to buy a little more time, but I couldn't keep pretending to have a stomach bug. Although…maybe I could pretend I was in heat. Anton had eluded to the fact that he was okay with me tending to my heat without their assistance. I didn't want to be with them when it hit. It would do nothing but forge a closer bond to them, one I still didn't want.

I didn't want that pack. I didn't want Bryan, Eric, Chris, or Anton to be my alphas. With the exception of Eric's indiscretion, they'd been nothing but kind to me. Sweet. Gentle. But they didn't call to my omega the way…

The way Kai did. Kai, who didn't feel he was good enough for me. Kai, who had called me a spoiled princess from day one. Kai, who didn't have a pack of his own.

Kai, who said he couldn't claim me but would give me every piece of him I needed until it was time for me to say goodbye.

Pushing from the side of the bed, I set my phone on the nightstand and left the room.

He was stretched out on the couch, one arm over his head, the other resting across his stomach. He wasn't hiding from me, wasn't on the patio or in the basement like he'd done since I'd fucked him on the couch. It had only gotten worse since I'd officially started courting the pack.

His eyes roamed me from head to toe and a tiny smile quirked up one corner of his mouth.

Glancing down at my clothes, I turned on my heel and headed

back to my room. I'd started the habit of dressing the part of a bonded omega. I'd worn the expensive clothing, done my hair and makeup, even wore flats or heels around the house just in case one of the pack wanted to see me.

Always be pleasing to the eye.

Be a good little omega.

Spoiled princess.

As long as I was in this house, away from prospective alphas, away from packs wanting to add the rare gem to their family, I wanted to simply be me. Just Sophie. Not the omega. Just me.

Stripping down to only my underwear, I tossed my bra into the hamper, rehung the blouse and designer jeans, set my shoes in the closet, then donned a pair of sweats and a tank top. It was getting a little cool for the tanks, but I could always wrap up in a blanket or pull a hoodie over top if I got chilly.

Or I could do what I really wanted and sprawl over Kai and soak up his body heat.

When I stepped back into the living room, Kai did the same slow perusal of my body then nodded with a smile.

"Better," he said in that deep, grumbly voice.

With a roll of my eyes, I shook my head and crossed the room, taking my place in the recliner and tucking my legs under me.

"Sorry about last night," I said after a few minutes of the two of us staring at the television screen.

"I'm not," he muttered without looking in my direction.

"It wasn't fair to you. Shoot, it wasn't fair to me." Or the pack. Technically, I was officially off the market, even if I didn't yet carry their marks.

But courting was as close to engagement as it got.

The TV suddenly went dark as Kai aimed the remote and turned it off, then sat up and turned to face me. "I meant what I said last night. I'll give you anything I can until…" He let the words trail off as though he was having a hard time voicing them. "I need to…I shouldn't have said that."

"Which part?" Was he now taking it back? Within seconds, he'd decided he couldn't give me the comfort I found only in his arms.

"I don't see you as a spoiled princess. I was lashing out. I…you…I shouldn't have said that."

A slow smile stretched across my face. His face stretched into a grin.

"I was jealous."

"Of me?"

"Of you. Of your life. Of your future…of the packs."

"Why the packs? You…you're not one of those guys who was ugly growing up and doesn't realize you grew into a super hot alpha, are you?"

Pink rushed his cheeks and warmed my freaking heart.

"I was jealous–" He cut himself off and pushed a hand through his hair, messing it. Dragging that same hand down his face, he smoothed his beard and a rumble of a growl rattled from his chest. "They get their choice of an omega. They get you."

"You've had me. Twice," I teased.

I knew what he meant. I knew he was trying to be serious, that he was putting his feelings out there, exposing himself for me to see. But his words were causing even more doubt and pain in my heart. Already, I was terrified of the future that my family had planned for me, that the pack was currently laying out for me.

In this house, with Kai, I could pretend I had a different life, that I was a different person.

Kai shifted in his seat, and he didn't bother hiding the fact that he was adjusting his growing erection.

"You know what I meant."

"I do," I said, the smile bleeding from my face as sorrow settled in my heart.

We were quiet for a few seconds. A few awkward seconds as though neither of us knew what to say next.

"Tell me about what you'd planned for the, for your…the thing you wanted to build. The organization."

I liked this distraction, even if it now seemed as though those plans were no better than the pages of a novel.

"If I had my way, and if I could execute it the way I'd planned while working on my studies, I would have a huge building, the kind with dozens of apartments. Temporary homes for displaced omegas, those who either didn't have a family to watch over them or those who'd escaped crappy situations. I would have all kinds of staff. I would have people who helped with furthering education for omegas, people like you who could teach them self-defense and how to protect themselves in public. There would be a medical facility with trained profession-als, maybe even scientists, who could help find long-term heat suppressants. We would provide birth control and scent blockers regardless of whether or not the omegas had the means to pay. Most of us aren't given the option to work after we present."

I'd been able to attend school but had finished my degree online after I'd perfumed in class and nearly sent the young alphas into rut. The choices laid out to me and my family was either online classes or expulsion.

"You've put a lot of thought into it," he said.

Nodding, I reached for the throw on the back of the recliner and laid it over my lap. "Since I presented. I didn't...my mom and siblings are all omegas. Did I ever tell you that?"

He shook his head, leaning forward to rest his elbows on his knees.

"They are the epitome of what omegas in our society are supposed to be. They're soft spoken, polite, never leave the house without looking perfect, and submissive. Don't get me wrong – it was nice growing up with money. But it was never part of my identity. I didn't care about the labels on my clothes like my mom or sister. Both siblings have already had pups and they're younger than me. I swear they courted and bonded with the first packs who showed any interest."

Packs my fathers had sought to pair with their children.

"I'm the black sheep," I said with a chuckle. "The old maid. That's why I'm here. The choices were either I agree to court packs, find my alphas, and live happily ever after, or I was out on the street. I have my degree, but that won't do a whole lot for me. Even the Omega Center doesn't care about my master's."

Kai's eyes stayed on my face the entire time I spoke. He didn't interject, didn't interrupt. Simply listened.

Waving my hand in the air, I leaned back in the seat. "It sounds like I'm playing poor little rich girl."

"No, it doesn't. I get it. More than I did when we met. You've been given no choice about your own life."

"Exactly," I said, jabbing a finger in his direction. "I'd thought...but you saw through their lies, through their bullshit. You are the first person in my life to be completely honest with me."

His wide shoulders rose and fell. "I've never been good at sugar coating. And I'm a terrible fucking liar."

"Tell me about you. Why did you go to work for Omega Rescue and Extraction?"

Kai grunted and sat back, his legs spread, his hands folded in his lap. "It seemed like the logical next step after the military."

"You were a soldier?"

He snorted, a scoffing sound. "I was a marine. There's a difference."

Holding my hands up, I widened my eyes and fought a smile. "Oops. Sorry. You were a *marine*?" I said, putting emphasis on the word.

"Yeah. Two tours overseas. I thought about law enforcement, but I had a couple buddies on ORE. One of them found his omega during a raid on a compound a few months back. He made the job sound bad ass. I applied, went through training, and had been working with my team for the past eight years."

Sadness entered his blue eyes, and he cleared his throat.

"Why...why aren't you working with your team now?"

I had a feeling I knew the answer, and felt terrible for voicing the question.

"I lost two of my teammates on that same raid. The remaining two of us have officially been displaced. Hence my placement with you."

"I'm sorry," I said, the words woefully inadequate.

Kai cleared his throat again and shook his head, waving his hand dismissively. "It's fine. You didn't know."

"Were you close?"

He was looking across the room and I wondered if he was replaying the night in his head. After a few seconds, he blinked rapidly and refocused his attention on me. "You become brothers when you work side by side. They weren't pack, but they were…they were my family."

Tossing the blanket off, I climbed from the recliner and crossed the space until I could straddle Kai's lap, resting my hands on his shoulders. "I'm so, so sorry."

I leaned forward and pressed a kiss to his forehead, then wrapped my arms around his shoulders and hugged him. It took a moment, but Kai wrapped his thick arms around my back and rested his head on my shoulder, letting me hold him.

Threading my fingers through his hair, I turned my head and pressed a kiss to the top of his head, lending him the little bit of comfort I could.

A soft purr vibrated against my chest as we held each other in complete silence.

Perhaps we were comforting each other. Perhaps we were soothing away the pain we felt in different ways.

Last night had been the change in our strained relationship. It was as though we'd both ripped open our chests to allow the other a peek inside. And I feared we would both be left raw, ragged, and bleeding in a matter of weeks.

Kai

I DIDN'T KNOW how long we sat like that with Sophie holding me, her scent wrapping around me like a blanket. Eventually, we'd stretched out on the couch, her back to my front, and dozed off while watching a movie.

Her breathing was slow and steady, my arm was draped over her waist, my knees lined against the backs of hers.

And my cock was cradled perfectly against her tight little ass.

Burying my face in her hair, I inhaled deeply, bringing all that floral sweetness into my lungs, hoping to keep some of it permanently, even after she was gone.

This was torture. I was falling hard for a woman I couldn't have.

Who the fuck was I kidding? I'd wanted her since her sassy little ass had walked through the door, all beauty and attitude.

Watching as she'd started to retreat into herself, watching as the fire and fight bled from her eyes, watching as she'd tried to mold herself into the perfect omega everyone expected her to be had nearly broken my heart.

If there was anything I could do to help her earn her freedom, I would do it in a heartbeat. I would sacrifice anything and everything to see her happy, to see her build her dream, to watch as she built something that would protect omegas, to give them a chance at a future without the threat of rutting alphas and packs trying to claim them.

Hugging her tighter, I smiled softly when she wiggled against me, the sweetest sigh escaping her lips.

"Don't move," she muttered sleepily. "I'm too comfortable."

Taking a chance, I moved my face through her hair until my lips made contact with the back of her neck.

She hummed in approval. "On second thought, feel free to move."

I chuckled as a purr started in my chest. Her hands gripped my forearms and tightened my arms around her.

Turning her head, she looked at me over her shoulder. "How long have we been asleep?"

With a shake of my head, I kissed the tip of her nose. "No idea. But the sun is down."

"Hmm," she hummed, unbothered by the fact we'd slept half the day away.

Her fingers trailed along my forearms, her nails scraping softly up and down.

Desire grew between having her cute little ass pressed against my growing dick and the feeling of her softly stroking along my arms.

I'd told her I would give her anything I had to give as long as we were together. But I needed to feel her, too. Our time was limited. Our connection was strong but would never go any further than these four walls.

Taking a chance, I kissed the back of her neck again, raising one hand to push her hair aside so I could nip and kiss along her shoulder. The exact place where I would leave my mark if I'd been born into a different life, if I'd been the kind of alpha her family would accept to bond with their daughter.

"Kai," she sighed, her hips rotating and pushing back against me.

One of my arms was trapped under her head, but I had full use of the other. I stroked my hand across her throat, running my fingers along the soft skin there. Then I let my hand run between her breasts, cupping one and smiling at the pebbled nipple pressing against my palm.

A hand landed on my hip and she tugged, encouraging me to rock against her and I obliged happily.

From this angle, I was the one feeling all the pleasure as my shaft was stimulated by her ass. I needed to hear her moans. I needed to feel her writhing against me. I needed to feel her cunt clenching around my cock.

Moving my hand further down her body, I slid my hand past her sweats and panties and through her slick coated folds. Already she was so wet for me, ready for my body, ready for me to stretch her.

"More," she whispered as she continued gyrating her hips.

She tugged at her sweats, shoving them down as far as she could reach. I hooked a foot in them and helped her tug her feet free.

When she tried to turn to free my cock, I stilled her with a hand on her shoulder.

"Not yet," I said, my lips against her ear.

She shuddered then moaned when I put my hand between her

thighs again, rubbing along her folds then circling her clit with a finger.

"You're going to kill me," she said on a breathy chuckle.

"What a way to go," I teased, nipping her earlobe.

Her fingers dug into the arm trapped under her shoulders as she pushed forward in an attempt for deeper, harder contact with my hand.

"Tell me, Sophie. Tell me what you want." I needed her to say the words. I needed to hear from her that she wanted me. I wasn't one of those alphas, one of the men in the pack who assumed I had full access to her body. I wanted her to give herself over to me freely.

"I want you, Kai. I want all of you."

The urge to shove my pants down my hips and slam into her pussy was nearly dizzying. But I wanted to draw our time out as much as possible since I had no idea how much longer I would have with this beautiful woman.

Dipping a finger into her drenched cunt, I clenched my teeth as her inner walls fluttered and nearly sucked my finger deeper inside.

Fuck it. I couldn't hold out much longer. Later. Another time I would take more time. I would spend hours tasting her, drinking down her release, kissing and licking every inch of her body.

Right now, I needed to feel her around me. I needed to feel that same fluttering and clenching around my dick.

With one hand, I awkwardly shoved my shorts down as far as I could to release my engorged and aching cock. My knot was full and swollen and throbbed to be inside of her. But that would be her choice.

Reaching between us, I positioned myself against her core and slowly pushed in, gripping her thigh to spread her legs for deeper penetration.

"Kai," she cried out on a long moan.

"You feel so good." I moaned as that purr continued to rattle through my chest.

Slowly, I pumped in and out of her, hooking her leg back over my hip so I could use my hand and fingers on her clit, so I could fondle her tits, roll her nipples between my finger and thumb.

"More. Please more," she begged, pushing back against me as she tried to take me deeper, as she tried to make me take her harder.

"Not yet, sweetheart. I want my princess falling apart and coating me in your slick before I give you my knot."

"Oh...my..." She pushed back again, riding me as I pumped into her.

The slow rhythm gradually turned frenzied. Reaching around her hip, I toyed with her clit, rubbing it and pinching it until her walls clenched my cock and she cried out, my name leaving her tongue and floating in the air, mixing with the scent of her perfume, of our pheromones.

"Come for me, princess. Come on my cock."

"Yes. Yes. Harder."

Gripping her hip for stability, I slammed into her harder, faster, the sounds of my hips clapping against her ass making my hunger climb.

"Knot. Please. I need your knot."

Hooking her thigh over my arm, I pushed forward hard until my knot stretched her pussy then popped inside, her walls clamping and clenching until I barked out with my own release, shooting jet after jet of hot cum into her.

"Kai. Yes. More. Please."

Tugging and rolling, I trapped her under my body, my chest against her back, her face turned on the pillow and exposing her throat.

My gums throbbed with the urge to latch on as I rutted inside of her, grunting as she came again, squeezing my knot until my balls tightened and I filled her with more of my release, explosions rocking through my body and fireworks flashing behind my closed lids.

"Fuck. Sophie." I moaned as aftershocks caused us to tremble and jerk against each other.

As I caught my breath, I rolled again so we were side by side. I couldn't keep all my weight on her while we waited for my knot to release us. I would crush her tiny body.

I'd thought I was falling for Sophie. But I'd been fooling myself. I was already so fucking in love with her.

And every time I felt her under my hands, under my body, I fell a little further.

I told her I would give her every part of me, anything she needed. I had just ripped another piece of my heart loose and left it inside of her. And hoped she would keep it safe when she was bonded to the pack.

I hoped she wouldn't forget about me when she was sitting in the lap of luxury, when her belly was swollen with the heir to the little empire that pack was building.

CHAPTER 11

Sophie

In the two days since I'd lied and said I was under the weather, I'd received calls from each of my fathers and had flowers delivered from the pack I was officially courting.

I'd also slept beside Kai, in his bed, both nights. We'd also *not* slept in his bed. And on the couch. And in the shower.

And on the kitchen table.

He'd had the idea to keep the blinds and curtains closed in case one of the pack happened to show up at the door.

Problem with them doing a pop in was the entire house smelled strongly of me and Kai. There was no way they wouldn't know that Kai and I had made love on more than one occasion.

And that was what we'd done. Multiple times. We were making love. I was falling so hard in love with a man I could never have.

My heart ached every time I thought about the day I would pack my belongings and leave this house. How was I supposed to build a life with the four alphas when my heart, mind, and body officially belonged to someone else?

Tears burned the backs of my eyes as I rinsed shampoo from my hair. I had to ignore them. I refused to let them fall. Not yet.

For the moment, I was going to enjoy every moment I had with Kai. I would grieve later. I would grieve what we could never have and keep the memory of our short time locked in my heart. Then I would play the role of dutifully, submissive omega to my four alphas. I would spread my legs and let them fill me with their seed and give them a family.

Sounds came from the kitchen after I dried off and dressed in a pair of leggings and a sweater. The weather was getting cooler and we'd yet to turn on the heater. I kind of liked it cooler in the house; it meant I could cuddle with Kai to stay warm. It meant I could smother myself in his scent, drag it into my lungs, sear it into my memory for later.

"Whatcha doin'?" I asked as I rounded the corner.

"Making you breakfast."

"I wasn't aware you could cook."

Why hadn't we done this from the beginning? We'd wasted so much time pretending to be different people, trying to keep our distance from each other.

But wouldn't that have made leaving that much harder?

"I'm a bachelor with no pack. Of course I can cook."

Sitting at the table, I leaned my chin on my hand and smiled as I watched the muscles in his back bunch as he moved around the kitchen. I loved when he went shirtless. I loved to ogle his chest, his shoulders, his strong arms.

And I really liked the way his bare skin felt on mine.

My phone chirped from my bedroom. "Damn it," I muttered, jumping from my seat and running to grab it before it went to voice-mail. "Hello?"

"Are you interested in meeting the other pack?" Daddy Johnathan. The last of my dads I was interested in talking to.

"I'm already courting a pack."

"Of four alphas. The other has eight. More money. More power."

Closing my eyes, I counted softly in my head and steadied my voice. "No. I'm already courting the others. I'm not interested in… eight alphas are too many. I don't care about the money or power."

"You could at least meet them. See if there's a better connection."

"I'm still under the weather. I think I have the flu or something," I lied.

"You don't sound too bad."

Shit. I probably should have forced more scratch or rasp into my voice. "I've been sleeping a lot. And my security brought some soup from a local shop."

"At least think about it. Eight alphas means more chances of pups. And more money and power means more comfort for you."

No. It meant more money and power for him, for my family.

"I'll think about it." It felt like I'd done nothing but lie to my family for the past few days. "But I really like this pack."

Johnathan sighed over the line as though I was putting him out.

"Did you bring this up to my other fathers? Does Daddy Jim know you're trying to talk me into skirting my responsibilities?"

If anything would get him to back off, that statement would do it. I was an omega with strict rules. And since I'd agreed to court the pack with Bryan, Chris, Eric, and Anton, my family had to respect the time it would take for them to decide whether I was their omega.

A growl rumbled through the phone. "Feel better. Get back to courting. We need to set a day and time for us to meet the alphas. I want to see the house and nest before they invite you into their home."

"Of course. I'll let you know when I'm feeling better."

"You do that."

He ended the call. No terms of endearments. No declarations of love. As I stared down at my phone, I racked my brain for a single time any living person had uttered those three words. I couldn't remember anyone ever telling me they loved me.

My mother loved me. At least, I believed she did. But even she'd never said those words to me, not in the time I could remember.

Instead of leaving the phone in my room and having to run back if someone called, I carried it with me and left it on the coffee table.

Kai had set plates on the table and was loading them with bacon, eggs, and pancakes.

"Quite a spread, Chef Kai," I teased.

He stopped, and I tilted back my head, accepting a kiss before he stepped away and smoothed a hand over my damp hair.

"Pack?" he said as he lowered onto his chair and lifted a forkful to his lips.

"What?"

Jerking his chin toward my phone, he chewed and swallowed. "They wondering if you're still indisposed?"

I chuckled at his choice of words and shook my head. "One of my dads. Johnathan. He's trying to talk me into meeting with another pack."

"You're courting one." I didn't miss the light growl in his words.

"Yep. But he wants me to meet with the pack of eight. I reminded him of my *duties* to the pack I already agreed to court."

Kai was quiet as he ate half his plate, then pushed it forward. I'd seen how much he could eat and wondered if he'd lost his appetite.

"Why is he interested in you meeting with eight fucking alphas?"

It was my turn to lose my appetite. "Apparently, they're loaded. Politicians. Law enforcement. Finance officers. In Johnathan's words, more power and money."

Kai's eyes dropped to the table where his finger traced a pattern in the wood and I could practically hear his thoughts. Power and money, two things he didn't have.

And he wasn't with a pack. Omegas were expected to pack up with at least three alphas. Anything less was seen as low on the social ladder, as though the omega wasn't desirable enough to earn the attention of a larger pack.

Personally, I would have been just as content falling in love with a beta. Or simply one alpha. Then living my life the way I wanted.

I wanted Kai. I wanted a future with the man who was suddenly having a hard time meeting my gaze.

For a brief moment, I tried to picture how a life with him would look. I imagined coming home after a long day at the center that I'd built for omegas and finding him lounging on our couch in a pair of sweats. Or naked. That would be even better.

I imagined myself with a rounded belly, Kai's pup growing inside of me. I wondered if our pup would have his black hair and blue eyes or my honey blonde hair and brown eyes. Maybe a combination of the two.

Shaking my head, I let those little fantasies fade like smoke on the wind. As fun as it was to daydream, it did nothing but cause that fissure in my heart to expand, to splinter further.

"How much longer do you think we have?" Kai asked, his voice so soft, so sad.

We. How much longer did *we* have?

When the tears welled in my eyes, I didn't have the energy to blink them away. "I don't know. If anyone shows up here, they'll smell us. They'll know. If I keep pretending to be sick, someone will show up at the door. And then my hand will be forced. Or I'll be completely out of options, out of a family, no pack, and homeless."

His mouth opened then shut. I knew he wanted to argue with me. I knew he wanted to tell me those things would never happen. But he knew there were no words that could make the situation any better.

"A week. Maybe two," I finally forced out.

His head nodded slowly, his eyes finally lifting to my face.

No words were spoken. But an understanding exploded between us.

I was on my feet the exact same moment as Kai lunged forward and swept his arm across the table, clearing it and laying me out like a buffet.

His hand shook as he struggled to strip me bare then buried his face between my thighs, licking me, eating me, devouring me until I was writhing and crying out, coming on his tongue.

There was no purr as he rose up my body, pressing kisses to my thighs, my hips, my stomach, leaving dampness from my slick, from my release.

Hands rough, he gripped my hips and jerked me forward until he could line the blunt head of his cock to my opening and thrust forward, filling me to the point his knot nudged my opening.

"Fuck, Sophie," he growled out, lowering until his chest pressed against mine, kissing me deeply, my taste on his lips, his scent on my tongue.

When he lifted his head, his beautiful blue eyes glimmered with unshed tears as he felt the same heartbreak and desperation that was splitting my heart and soul apart.

Kai

WE HADN'T BOTHERED DRESSING after our hurried and frenzied love making on the kitchen table. The mess of eggs and syrup was still on the floor. I would clean it later. For now, I needed to feel Sophie in my arms. I needed to intoxicate myself with her scent. It was a punishment, torture, but what I needed.

Because soon, I would no longer have the chance to feel her against my body, to taste her sweet release, to tease my nose with her floral candied scent.

"After you've moved in with the pack, there's a good chance I won't see you again," I said, swallowing hard as emotion clogged my throat.

She nodded, her hair tickling my chin as she kept her face tucked into my throat.

"I don't have the right, but I'll need to know you're okay. And I need you to know I'll be there for anything. If these guys…if at any point the pack isn't what you want, please know I'll be there to help in every way I can."

She sniffed but didn't speak.

"I'm going to invite a couple friends over. They have an omega who…" I huffed a laugh. "Well, she grew up believing she was beta and presented late. She's a firecracker like you."

She chuckled at that, her body shaking lightly in my arms.

"I want you to form a friendship with Violet. Keep her number locked in your phone. I don't know those alphas, but most won't be happy with you having the number of another alpha. It might have been different if I was beta, but…"

"Evergreen."

I pulled back and tucked my chin to try to see her face. When she looked into my eyes, I felt my heart begin to shatter piece by piece. Her eyes were welled with tears and her cheeks were damp.

"That first time we went to the pack's house, you said I should have a signal or code word in case I wanted to leave."

I huffed a soft laugh but couldn't bring myself to smile. "Yeah. Evergreen. If anything goes wrong and you can't come out and ask for help, text that word to Violet. She'll let me know immediately. Even if I have to bring the entire force of ORE with me, I'll make sure you're out of there and safe."

"And then my family will find another pack to pawn me off on."

Stay with me. I'll take care of you. I'll be your pack.

Those were selfish thoughts. I knew she didn't want to be packed with those alphas. And I could see how she felt about me in her eyes now. But I also knew what was expected of her, could see the fear of being cut off from her family all over her pretty face.

Not only was I not good enough, but I would never *be* enough. One man. Not a pack. Nothing I could offer her that would ever rival big houses or fancy jewelry or the security of a larger pack.

"When?" she asked and sniffled. Pushing to a sitting position, she turned so she was resting against my chest but was no longer hiding her face against my throat.

"Sooner the better. I'll put in a call and see when they can come. You okay with a house full of alphas? There are four of them. But they're no threat to you. Their omega is friends with another coworker, a beta, if you want him as a buffer from all the alpha hormones."

"We could have a little party," she said with a forced and teary smile. "Yeah."

Except we wouldn't be able to head out for supplies. Because she was supposed to be in bed sick. If anyone saw the extra car in the driveway, it could be explained away as ORE business. I was, after all, a member of one of the most elite groups of law enforcement.

"You sure this is cool?" Andrei asked as he stepped inside with his omega and the rest of the pack filing right behind.

"Absolutely," Sophie answered.

She and Violet instantly rushed to each other, talking, laughing, and becoming fast friends.

While they were distracted, I jerked my head toward the patio, motioning for the alphas to follow me.

"Wilder coming?" I asked. Violet and the beta had become friends, but her alphas were still leery of letting another man so close to her, especially when she was near her heat.

"Nah. He's working tonight," Liam said. "Your omega is–"

"Not my omega," I said, cutting him off before I could let the words sink any further into my heart.

Frowns and looks were exchanged before they all turned their attention to me.

I laid it all out, told them everything. I had known Andrei the longest. Mac, too. But I didn't exactly consider them besties as the girls would say. But I trusted them. I trusted them with this secret as much as I trusted them with my life.

"You want her," Chase said softly.

"Yeah." I pushed a hand through my hair. "But she has a pack sniffing after her. Her parents chose them. She thinks she has maybe a week before they'll move her into their home. But…something doesn't sit well with me."

"Well, no. You're in love with an omega who's courting a pack of alphas," Liam said.

Mac cuffed him along the back of his head.

"They tell her what she wants to hear. She has all these dreams and shit. They had her convinced they would finance this business idea she has, but finally admitted they were simply placating her. We've seen the worst sides of packs. I just…I have a favor to ask."

I told them about the plan Sophie and I had come up with about the omegas becoming friends, about Sophie texting the code word if she found herself in trouble.

"Anything we can help with you know we have your back. Hers, too," Andrei said, his thick arms crossed over his chest.

Of the four, he looked like someone to be avoided in a dark alley with his ink covered body and piercings. He might have looked scary, but he was a good dude, a good soldier, and I'd seen how gentle he was with the omegas we'd rescued through the years.

"You could tell her how you feel. Join our pack," Chase offered.

With a shake of his head, he glanced through the glass doors to check on the women.

"No. She needs stability. And that's not something I can give her. I lost two of my team. I could be next. I won't bond her only for her to have to bury me before either of us hits forty."

The mood turned somber as the alphas around me turned and looked at their omega chatting with Sophie. I was sure they'd thought the same thing since they'd claimed Violet. I was sure they feared not returning to her every time they were sent on a mission.

But losing one, or even two of them…she might survive that. It would just be me and Sophie.

While I appreciated the offer of Sophie and I joining their happy little pack, I couldn't stomach the idea of any of these alphas touching her.

And yet…I would be handing her over to four men who would touch her, taste her, fuck her, and knot her. They would fill her with their pups. They would go to bed with her in their arms every night and wake up to her face every morning.

Fuck. One week. If we were lucky. I needed to get my fill of the most beautiful woman I'd ever met in my life in such a short period of time.

And then I would have to let her go.

CHAPTER 12

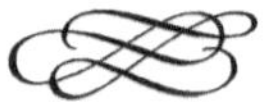

Sophie

I touched the brush to my under eyes, setting the concealer with powder. There was no amount of makeup that would hide the swelling from the hours of crying I'd done last night.

It had been eight days since Kai had invited his friends over. Eight days since I'd locked Violet's number in my phone.

And I'd received the call yesterday that I would be picked up by a car and delivered to the pack's home to finish our courting. They would be given six months to decide whether they would bond me, whether they would leave their mark on my shoulder, tying us together forever.

I was dressed in yet another new dress that had been delivered yesterday. The label alone told me one of my fathers had spent a pretty penny on it. Of course he did. They would want to make sure the gift was wrapped in only the best.

My chest ached. My room smelled heavily of Kai and me. I had made sure to use as many scent blocking body products as possible in hopes of hiding our extracurricular activities.

We had already made plans to have my things waiting outside in hopes of keeping whoever picked me up from stepping inside and learning that I wasn't such a good little omega after all.

Kai and me...last night would be seared in my mind, in my heart, on my soul for eternity.

When I hung up the phone, tears instantly welled and fell over my lashes. I didn't have to say a word. Kai knew our time was up. He'd rushed across the room and dragged me into his arms, crushing me to his chest.

His head dipped and buried in the crook of my neck, inhaling my essence, his lips brushing across my pulse point, pressing to my cheeks, my jaw, my eyelids, my forehead, anywhere he could reach before finally claiming my mouth.

And that was exactly what he'd done. He'd claimed my mouth the way he'd already claimed my heart. Our tongues danced and dueled, and struggled for dominance.

Our hands battled as we stripped every piece of clothing from each other, leaving a trail of fabric. The nest. I wanted to be in the nest with Kai. I wanted to leave some piece of us behind, even if I knew in the back of my mind every hint of our existence would be wiped away by some anonymous cleaning crew.

Kai touched, kissed, and licked every dip and valley of my body as though trying to commit every inch to memory. I knew the feeling. After he made me cry out and come on his tongue, I returned the favor.

After tonight, I would belong to practical strangers. My body would no longer be mine. My life would no longer be mine.

His hand was wrapped in my hair as I took his length into my mouth, swallowing as much as I could until I gagged. The drip of precum at his slit was sweet on my tongue and I wanted to savor it, brand it into my heartbeat.

With so much urgency, he pulled my head up and rolled us until he was on top of me, pushing my thighs open and slipping his cock into me with ease.

My body was made for him. His for me.

He was slow at first, gentle, his hips making circles as his hand stroked through my hair, cupping my cheek as he kissed me deeply, our tastes mingling on our tongues.

Need took over until he was pumping hard and fast and I fell apart, covering his cock in my release, the slippery sound mixing with our moans, his grunts, our flesh slapping together.

"Please," I begged as tears trailed down my temples to soak my hair.

Burying his face in my neck, his pushed hard, giving me his knot, filling me with his heat, and whispered, "I love you. I love you so fucking much." His voice was deep, raspy, choked with emotion.

A sob shook me at his words, at the loss I felt as they fell from his tongue.

"I love you, Kai. I'll love you forever."

I HADN'T LEFT my room since I woke this morning. I couldn't face him. I didn't regret telling him how I felt. And I didn't regret hearing those same words from him.

But I wasn't quite ready to say goodbye. I had less than an hour before I left this house and walked out of his life. Less than an hour before I became someone I'd never wanted to be and lived a life that wasn't of my choosing.

Hair and makeup perfect, clothes impeccable, bags packed, and then there was nothing to do but wait. I could go and curl into Kai's arms, let him hold me for our remaining time together.

But that would not only make things worse when it was time to go, it would leave his scent all over me.

Stop being a coward.

Pulling the door open, I began to set my bags outside the door, then stopped short when I spotted Kai in the hallway, leaned against the wall, his thick arms crossed over his chest.

His eyes were puffy, too. We'd both cried as we'd made love, cried until we'd fallen asleep in the nest tangled around each other.

And then I'd cried as I had washed his scent away. From where I stood, I couldn't detect my signature on him anymore, either. He'd done the same and erased any evidence of our short life together from his skin.

"I'll take the bags outside," he said, his eyes barely ghosting over my face.

I wanted nothing more than to stop him, to demand he hold me. But then we'd both have to wash our scents away again.

It was time to rip the band-aid off and accept the fact I'd experienced the greatest love in such a short period of time. I'd experienced in a few weeks what some would never experience in their lifetime.

And I was thankful to Kai for that.

I waited in the living room as Kai set my bags on the porch as we'd planned. He took a seat on the couch, so I took my place on the recliner I tended to occupy.

"Will you be okay?" I asked softly.

He huffed a laugh, but it held zero humor and his lips didn't so much as quirk at the corners.

"I'm worried about you," he said. Turning his face to me, he leaned forward and rested his elbows on his knees, dropping his head as though it was too heavy for his neck to hold up. "Promise me, Sophie. Promise me that if anything goes wrong, if they mistreat you, scare you, force you into anything you don't want, you'll contact Violet immediately. I'll kick down the door myself if I have to. I *will* get you out."

"And then the whole thing starts over again," I said. "My family won't be content until I'm packed with the cream of the crop," I said, using the words he'd said in the very beginning of our stay together.

"I shouldn't have said that."

"You apologized. You explained. You're forgiven," I said.

Keeping this distance from him was slowly breaking more slivers of my heart away until it felt as though I was becoming hollow.

My phone chimed, and I squeezed my eyes shut at the first prickling of tears. I heard the couch squeak under his weight, heard the blinds move.

"The car is here," he said, his voice deep and guttural.

When I opened my eyes, Kai was stepping through the front door to carry my bags to the car that was waiting to drag me away.

"Get it together," I muttered to myself. I couldn't cry my makeup off. I couldn't show up to the pack house a blubbering mess.

It was time to slip the mask back into place and pretend I was someone else.

With one more glance around the house, I tried to commit every minute of my time here to memory, tried to picture every single place where Kai and I had made love.

And then squared my shoulders and walked on my four-inch heels through the front door.

The driver stood outside the back door waiting as Kai loaded my bags into the trunk.

He nodded at the driver as he passed, then locked eyes with me for the briefest second.

"Can you give us a minute?" I called to the driver. "I want to thank Mr. Janse for his service."

"Yes, ma'am," the driver said, turning his back as though to give us a modicum of privacy.

Kai stopped at the bottom of the stairs, tilting his head back to look into my face.

All the things I wanted to say stayed lodged in my throat. Finally, after a few seconds, I smiled softly. "I love you, Kai. I'll love you forever," I whispered the same words I had told him last night.

"I'll love you forever. And I'm here for anything you could ever need."

His eyes glimmered, but he rubbed at them as though the sun was bothering him.

Keep it together. I can't let my emotions take over.

He stepped out of the way as I descended the steps, taking the chance to graze my fingers along his as I passed.

The driver opened the door when he heard my heels clacking along the sidewalk announce my approach.

Once encased in the backseat with the tinted windows, I stared at Kai's back. It was as though he refused to turn, refused to see me taken away.

Just as the car passed the third house and I could barely make out where he stood, Kai turned and watched as I was driven out of his life. I saw his head tilt back, saw his mouth open, saw the pain in his face, even if I couldn't hear the bellow of pain and rage that left his mouth.

My arm was hooked through Eric's as he gave me a tour of the house. He'd apologized several times for his previous behavior and was nothing short of a gentleman now.

The other three alphas followed us closely as they made sure I memorized the layout of the house, introduced me to the staff, then showed me to my quarters. And my nest.

"Has your cycle hit yet?" Chris asked.

The immediate sassy answer bubbled up, but I bit it back and smiled at him over my shoulder. "Not yet."

And not if I could secretly get my hands on suppressants. I'd heard there were situations when an omega wouldn't go into heat if she weren't with the right alphas. Maybe if I could stave off my cycle, they would give up and demand my parents remove me.

But then what? Then I would be handed off to the pack of eight alphas, if they were still available. Or another group. It would go on and on until my fathers made sure I was with a wealthy pack and carrying a pup and locked into a life just like my mom's, just like my sister's, just like my brother's.

It was best to simply let nature take over, let these men rut me, let them breed me, and accept that this was all I had to look forward to.

"Feel free to change anything in your quarters or your nest. We can either bring in a designer or we can go shopping. Anything and everything can be delivered, too," Anton said from the doorway of my bedroom.

It was pretty, I supposed. A little on the girly side. Actually, *a lot* on the girly side with pastel colors and lacy coverlets. It smelled of chemical cleaners as though they'd tried to erase a scent.

Of a former omega? Of women they'd bedded in this very room?

It didn't matter. There was zero jealousy over the fact these men had fucked other women in the past. Hell, I didn't care if they continued to sleep around if it meant they would have less time and energy for me.

I would do as I was born to do. I would submit to their rules, I would spread my legs and give them heirs. I would dress pretty and smile at the galas and benefits and parties where we would bump elbows with all the powers that be.

"Your fathers had the rest of your belongings delivered last week, but feel free to move things around the way you want them."

Last week. When I'd pretended to be sick. When I had yet to set a date when I would officially move in with the pack to consummate our courtship.

"Would you like to change clothing? Get more comfortable? We stocked the bathroom with as much as we could think you might want. The tub is more than spacious," Anton said with hunger in his eyes. "Or you could shower before dinner."

Eric squeezed my arm closer to his side and dipped his head, his nose running up the side of my neck. I shuddered, wishing I was anywhere but here.

He took it as encouragement. "So beautiful," he cooed, kissing my neck. "Would you like one of your alphas to join you?"

Swallowing hard, I forced a smile and turned to look up into his face. "I'm still a little weak from being sick. Would it be okay if I took a little nap? Then I'll shower and come down so we can spend some time together. Get to know each other better."

"There are way more fun ways to get to know each other," Chris teased with a waggle of his brows.

Had I not experienced my time with Kai, I might have laughed at his joke. I might have even invited him into the shower with me, gotten to know him on a more carnal level.

Instead, I feigned the submissive omega and batted my lashes. "I would hate to give you anything less than one hundred percent of myself."

"Such a perfect little omega," Chris said.

Good little omega.

I wasn't sure how long I could put off laying down for these men. I wasn't sure how long the alphas would allow their sweet little omega to keep them out of my bed. But I would hold off for as long as I could.

At least until ice began to fill the cracks left in my heart from leaving Kai.

Each man pressed a kiss to my cheek before leaving my side, pulling the door to my bedroom closed behind them.

Turning slowly, I sought my personal items that had supposedly been delivered. There on the dresser was my jewelry box that I knew contained diamonds, pearls, and other precious stones I'd been gifted through my life.

In the corner of the room was a tall mirror that I'd used countless times to check my outfit. Beside it was an antique chair that I'd inherited from my maternal beta grandmother.

The room was massive, bigger than the living room at the house I'd shared with Kai. Beside the nest was a door that led to a walk-in closet. So much of what I'd left behind was now hanging neatly in rows.

Drawers in the dresser contained underwear, pajamas, and t-shirts. All that was left was to unpack the bags I'd brought with me.

This was my home now. This was my room. That was my bed. A bed that someone would eventually want to share with me.

Would it be terrible if I closed my eyes when they touched me and pretended it was Kai, pretended it was Kai's hands on me, pretended it was Kai's weight pushing me into the mattress?

Or would that cheapen what we'd had, taint the memory of our short love story?

Sitting on the edge of the bed, I stared at the room without seeing it. I'd washed his scent from me, but that didn't mean I couldn't feel Kai in every beat of my heart.

We'd wasted so much time. We'd pretended to be other people. Pretended to dislike each other. We'd kept each other at arm's length.

And now it was too late.

CHAPTER 13

Sophie

The alphas sat around the table with mugs of coffee in their hands when I turned the corner. They were dressed in office wear – button up shirts, ties, slacks, their jackets hanging over the backs of their chairs.

And I knew they would expect me to be ready for the day before letting them set eyes on me.

I was dressed in a pair of slacks and a sweater that hugged my waist, cinched with a belt, the front dipping to reveal cleavage. My hair was curled, the sides pulled back and away from my face with a pretty clip. Makeup was minimal but perfect. I'd already showered and used one of the fruity smelling body washes they'd left for me.

My feet were squeezed into a pair of leather pumps that clicked against the marble floor, catching the men's attention.

Anton cleared his throat, a frown creating a tiny crease between his brows.

"We haven't really had time to discuss what all of us expect of you and what you expect of us. But we don't employ a morning staff. We want to give you time to get accustomed to your new surroundings, but we ask that you have breakfast ready so we don't waste time and end up late to work."

"Of course. I apologize."

Was I supposed to wake up to the sun? Because there was no alarm clock in my bedroom.

"Ignore him. Take your time getting acquainted with your new home. A week should be enough for you to figure out where everything is," Bryan said with a wink, as though his words would make the situation any better.

"Would you like dinner ready when you get home?" I bit out, my cheeks almost sore from the forced smile.

"Don't be silly. The staff usually arrives around noon. They'll take care of dinner. They are also responsible for the housework, things like laundry, dusting, all that. And you'll see the lawn crew periodically throughout the week, so don't be scared if you see strangers outside," Eric said.

"So…what would you like me to do throughout the day?"

"Whatever you wish. We have an extensive library. The driver can take you into town if you want to go shopping or meet with a friend for brunch. And we were serious when we said we support your goal of building a facility for omegas, as long as you're still here when we get home," Bryan offered.

"Has anyone shown her the nursery?" Anton asked.

He'd seemed so sweet that day. His scent still wasn't unappealing to me, even though I wanted to be anywhere but here. But now, it felt as though layers were being peeled away from his mask and I was seeing a carbon copy of my fathers.

"I'm sure she'll find it. Explore the house some more today. Our bedrooms are open to you. Feel free to pleasure yourself in any of them. Leave your scent around the house. It'll help our bond. And maybe encourage your heat to come sooner rather than later. We're ready to increase the size of our family," Chris said.

Smile still plastered on my face, I swallowed back the bile. "A bonding ceremony?" I asked.

They were talking about getting me pregnant before we had even completed the bond.

"We'll hire a company to plan that. Please feel free to give them your input, tell them how your perfect ceremony would look. We want the ceremony to be as beautiful as you could dream."

I didn't dream of bonding ceremonies. I dreamed of being loved and cherished. Just like I had dreamed of living a life of my own choosing.

Now, I dreamed of finding a way to become numb to the ache in my chest.

I WANDERED the halls of the house for hours, looking over the titles of the books on the shelves, running my fingers over the smooth wood of the furniture, perusing the snack selection in the pantry.

Each of the alphas' rooms were similar yet different. Although the difference might very well have been chalked up to their scents. They all appeared to prefer rich, masculine colors, the complete opposite of the pastel colors they'd used to decorate the omega's room.

The men each had a bed big enough to fit several of us at once. Where my room and the nest had a chemical smell, I detected others in each of the rooms, clean scents of betas. They had definitely entertained women in their bedrooms.

And still, I couldn't find even an ounce of jealousy.

Hope. That was what I felt. Hope that maybe they would continue having affairs and pretend I was nothing more than an adornment, a decoration for the house, an accessory when they were in public.

Only one door remained closed in the long hallway, the last room to explore. And I knew before I opened the door what I would find.

My heart stuttered and a strange longing settled in my heart when my eyes swept over the crib, the rocking chair in the corner, the soft toys sitting on shelves beside children's books.

I had thought about motherhood. Of course I had. I was an omega.

But I had always thought it would be on my time. Or rather I'd *hoped* it would be on my time. If the alphas had their choice, this room would be used in a year.

An image of Kai hovering over my shoulder, beaming down at a blonde baby with his striking blue eyes squeezed my chest and I had to leave the room, pulling the door closed behind me so hard it slammed.

"Ma'am?" a female asked, and I started with a squeak, slapping a hand over my chest.

A sweet older beta stood with her hand on the handle of a vacuum, her eyes wide.

"I'm so sorry. I didn't mean to scare you."

"No. It's fine," I said, smiling at her and hoping to reassure her. "I forgot you guys would be here around noon."

"If you're hungry, I could make you lunch."

Waving my hand, I brushed her off. "I'm fine. Not hungry yet." Or at all since I'd stepped into this house. "I'll find something if I change my mind."

Leaving the housekeeper gaping after me, I hurried out of the hallway and to the library. I could do anything I wanted, according to my alphas, as long as it consisted of being in the house, looking pretty, or being chaperoned if I left the house.

As far as I could tell, I'd ventured into every room of the house except the basement. If it was anything like the one at the house where I'd stayed with Kai, it wouldn't be much to look at and I wasn't exactly known to lift weights.

The image of the first time I'd approached Kai as he'd pummeled the huge bag hanging from the ceiling, his chest bare and glistening with sweat sent warmth through my body. And an ache in my heart.

I refused to ever let go of the few memories we'd made or erase him from my heart. But perhaps it was time to find a way to stop dwelling constantly on what I had lost. On what *we* had lost.

My life was completely different now. I had a role to play. And I couldn't do that if I sunk into depression.

Squaring my shoulders, I let my eyes wander over every single title of the books on the shelves, trying to find something to occupy my time until my future alphas arrived home. I wasn't given a time to expect them, but I knew from my time with my own family that they would expect me to look the part, to be dressed as someone who belonged in this ridiculous house.

There were absolutely no romance novels on the shelves. Not even horror or fantasy. In fact, the collection looked more as though they were placed there for appearance rather than enjoyment.

I still hadn't spotted a television, not even in my own bedroom. Surely these guys enjoyed downtime in front of the boob tube. Who didn't binge shows or watch movies?

Eventually, I officially ran out of things to keep myself occupied.

Wandering back up to my bedroom, I lowered to the foot of the mattress and looked around. They had said I could change things up, decorate it how I wanted. Since I couldn't leave the house without an escort, I would have to wait until they came home to discuss hiring a consultant. I wanted this place to feel like mine, to feel as though I belonged here instead of feeling as though I was a stranger in what was supposed to be my permanent home.

My feet dangled off the end as I kicked them and tried to picture how I would want the room to change. All the girly pastels had to go. The lace, too. It was like they'd prepared the room for a teen girl instead of an adult omega. And what would they have done if their omega had been male? They couldn't possibly think every single one of us liked feminine crap.

Not that I didn't mind soft blankets and pillows. But I was into warmer colors, natural colors and textures. I liked feeling as though I was on a beach somewhere or walking through the woods instead of feeling as though I'd fallen straight into the playroom of a six-year-old girl.

The room at the halfway house was neutral if not plain. It was for temporary use so there wasn't much in the way of décor or art. But it had felt like home, even if only for the few weeks I'd been there.

Would someone have come in and cleared our scents away by

now? Would they have doused the place in scent blockers? Erased any evidence of the deep connection that had taken place there?

The whir of a vacuum sounded from somewhere deep in the house. My only company was hired staff who apparently did their best to stay out of sight and had appeared a little stressed that they'd ended up in the same wing when I'd found the nursery.

I was alone. And it would be like this every workday. Possibly on the weekends if my alphas were social butterflies. I knew there would be parties. I knew I would be expected to dress in designer clothes and cling to my alphas' arms as they paraded around their rare gem, bragging that they not only scored an omega, but the daughter of a wealthy family.

My phone was cool in my hand; the only numbers in it were Violet's and my family's. I could always text Violet, see if she would be up to having lunch soon. It would be nice to have a friend. And it didn't hurt that she had a tiny connection to Kai that I could cling to, even if it was pathetic and made me feel as though I only wanted to further the friendship to use her in hopes of catching some gossip about how he was doing.

And whether he'd moved on.

Scooting backward, I laid on the mattress, folding my hands over my stomach, and stared up at the stark white ceiling. I was bored. I hated being bored. As soon as the guys got home, I'd find out whether there was a TV. If not, I'd ask for one, even if it stayed in my room. And I needed access to some online shopping sites so I could order a few books.

Master's degree and I was relegated to being a housewife. And I didn't even have a house to clean since they outsourced that to their staff. I was expected to make breakfast, but the rest of the meals would apparently be prepared for us.

My memories of my mother were of her raising us. She'd had her hands full with three kids. She'd been kept busy.

If the pack had their way, that would be my life in a year. Unless I could find a way to suppress my heat. Or sneak some birth control. Maybe I would get lucky and they'd think I was barren. I wasn't sure if they would decide I was defunct and send me away or if they would keep me around while trying to find another way to fill the house with pups.

I wouldn't wish that on anyone.

My eyes grew heavy as I laid there trying to pretend I had a different life. Trying to pretend I could make my current situation a happy one. Trying to find something, some sliver left in my heart that I could give my new alphas.

And just like I knew would happen, Kai's face teased me in my dreams.

A SMILE TEASED at the corners of my lips as fingertips floated over my shins, up to my thighs. The mattress dipped below me as those same fingertips raised to push hair from my face. Roasted marshmallow. Not fresh baked cookies.

Eyes flying open, I blinked a few times as Eric's face came into view and my vision cleared.

"Taking a little nap?" he asked, his touch light as he stroked a hand down my face, down my neck, and over my shoulder.

"I wasn't sure what to do. I got..." My cheeks heated. "I got bored and laid down for a second. I didn't realize I'd fallen asleep."

"You must have been having a good dream. You were smiling when I came in."

It was a very good dream, but not one I would ever tell Eric about.

His eyes lowered and trailed over my body, the invisible caress making me antsy. I knew it was only a matter of time before each of them laid a claim to my body, even before the bonding ceremony, before they latched their teeth onto my shoulder to leave their permanent marks on my skin.

"The others will be home soon. You should get yourself cleaned up for dinner."

But he didn't rise, didn't roll off the side of the bed. Instead, his fingers began to take the path he'd started with his eyes, gently grazing over the swell of each of my breasts, down my stomach to toy with the waist of my slacks, barely dipping below the line.

Forcing a smile on my face, I lifted onto my elbows. "I was thinking…" I started, looking up at Eric through my lashes in hopes of looking coy.

"Yes?"

"It would be kind of romantic if we all waited. You know, until the bonding ceremony. Just think of the flirting we can do in the meantime. I've always thought people who waited until they were fully committed were so romantic. It would be so beautiful."

For a second, I feared he'd heard the tremble in my voice or the bitter turn of my scent as anxiety rose.

"Romantic," he said, his fingers popping the button of my pants then pulling down my zipper.

He lowered until his face hovered over my panties and inhaled deeply, humming his approval.

"I think I can do that. I can't speak for your other alphas. But I do want you carrying my scent."

He pulled his cock from his pants and rolled onto his side so he was facing me.

"Undress for me. I don't want to ruin those pretty clothes."

Swallowing back the bile, I lifted the sweater over my head then pushed my slacks down my legs, folding them and setting them at the end of the bed.

"Lie back for me."

I did as I was told and stared into Eric's face as he lifted onto his knees and began to pull on his cock in a frantic rhythm, almost like he was nearing rut. There would be nothing I could say to stop him if he climbed on top of me, if he ripped my underwear away and took his omega the way an alpha was permitted.

He never looked me in the eye, instead staring at my breasts, my lacy underwear, and my thighs before grunting and spilling his release across my stomach, some hitting my arm and mattress.

"Fuuuck," he groaned out, dropping back onto his heels as he tucked himself away.

His hand was a little too rough as he dragged it over my stomach, rubbing his scent into my skin. Just like I'd done that night with Kai when I'd wanted nothing more than to carry his signature with me, to envelope myself in it so I could feel safe and sleep and forget the fact I was being forced with men I didn't want.

"Don't shower yet. Get dressed. Fix your hair. Then come down. I want your alphas to smell me all over you."

He bent over and pressed his lips to mine in an oddly gentle kiss before practically bounding off the bed and leaving me lying alone, his cum cooling on my skin.

This was my life. This was all that was left of me. And soon, the four alphas would do as they pleased with every inch of my body and every aspect of my life.

CHAPTER 14

Sophie

*R*ushing through my morning routine, I didn't have time to curl my hair *and* do my makeup. So after making sure my face was perfect, I twisted my hair into a pretty bun at the base of my neck, dressed quickly, and practically sprinted for the kitchen. I still didn't know what time it was, but I'd heard their voices through the walls and had heard them moving around the house.

It had been a week and I'd yet to make it to the kitchen before them.

Anton leaned against the counter as I entered. Eric, Chris, and Bryan glanced at me as I stepped onto the cool tile floor, matching looks of disappointment on their faces.

How had I thought them handsome? They weren't bad looking, but the more time I spent with them, the faster their masks were dropping, and I was seeing the cold, detached looks in their eyes. They no longer had to court me, not really. I was all but purchased. The only thing left was the ceremony and the bites.

"We've given you a week. You're almost an hour later," Anton said, dumping the contents of his mug into the sink and setting it on the counter.

"I don't have a clock in my room. Am I supposed to wake up to the sun?"

Something darkened in Anton's eyes. A muscle jumped in his jaw the same time his warm paper scent turned to something ashy and bitter.

And then his arm snaked out and he grabbed me by my bicep, his grip tight enough to leave marks.

I nearly tripped over my own feet as he dragged me from the kitchen without a single protest or growl from my future alphas.

"Sit," he said, shoving me onto the couch and hovering over me. "I'm not sure what happened in the time from when you left your house to when you arrived here, but I am not some low life alpha who allows my omega to disrespect me. Don't think for a second we didn't scent that security guard all over you. We're fully aware you were spreading your legs for him. Did we say a fucking word?"

A tremble started in my body and worked its way to my toes. I thought I had been careful. I thought I'd cleansed my clothing and skin of any hints of our time together.

Anton leaned down, his hands landing on the cushions on either side of my head. "You will learn, one way or another, to be a true omega. Eric told me you've requested we wait to consummate until the bonding ceremony. I will give you that. And not a day longer. But you will do as you're told. You will be down here, coffee and breakfast made, before I put my foot on the steps in the morning."

Anger and fear warred inside of me. When he backed away, I pushed to my feet and did my best to remember who the hell I was.

"I don't have a clock. I need an alarm clock if you expect me to have your breakfast on the table in time."

He glared down at me, and I fought the urge to rub the throbbing in my arm where he'd manhandled me.

"I've agreed to be your omega. I've agreed to be part of your pack. But I did not agree to be your servant."

One moment, Anton was glaring down into my face. The next, he swung and backhanded me, hitting my cheek hard enough for me to see stars. I wasn't sure I'd ever been struck before, nothing more than a swat on the bottom as a child.

Or the spanking I'd received from Kai.

"You didn't need to agree to anything. Your father made the decision for you. *We* made the decision for you. We can all have a very good life together. But if I have to beat that spirit out of you, so help me I will. I'll spend every day of the rest of your life teaching you how to be a good omega to your alphas."

Touching a trembling hand to my cheek, I stared silently up into his face with wide eyes. He'd struck me. He'd hit me. He'd threatened me. He'd threatened to beat me if I didn't comply.

My father made the decision for my life. Anton and his pack made the decision for my life.

And all I could do was fight the tears that welled in my eyes at all the things I would never experience, all the things I'd lost before I'd ever had them.

Chair legs scraped against tile as the men stood. They filed through the house, barely glancing in my direction as they tugged on their suit jackets.

"Eric said you've requested a television set. I'll have one delivered this afternoon. But I suggest finding something more productive with your time than sitting around all day and getting out of shape. You have a role to play. And that includes being attractive on my arm when we make our first public appearance." Anton looked as though there was more to say, but he shook his head as though I was the one who'd done wrong, turned his back on me, and stomped from the house.

The front door slammed shut, and I dropped heavily onto the couch, wrapping my arms around my middle and gasping for air as panic ripped through me like a tornado.

This was my life. I either allowed them to mold me into a completely different person or...

Tears spilled down my cheeks, clearing the makeup I'd carefully applied before rushing downstairs. I would have to reapply it before they got home. I would have to touch up my hair before they saw me again.

I would have to hide the bruise I knew would form on my cheek before I let them lay eyes on me later in the day.

A LARGE FLAT screen television was delivered later in the afternoon as Anton had promised. The men had carried it to my room and installed it, attaching it to my wall and showing me how to use the remote to navigate through the various streaming services.

I'd made sure to conceal the evidence of my abuse before the betas had arrived. Not because I feared they would tell anyone, but because I was humiliated. Ashamed. I didn't want anyone to see who I'd become in the short time I'd been with this pack.

The trembling finally stopped a couple hours later, but my nerves were still strung tight. Anxiety burned my stomach and I paced the house, terrified to be caught alone, terrified to be caught being lazy, terrified of doing anything wrong even if I had no idea what exactly these alphas expected of me other than to do as they said when they said it.

The only expectations they'd laid out was to have their breakfast ready, to be pretty, and to give them babies.

Now, I was walking on pins and needles, wondering what else I was missing, what else I should do. What if I made another mistake and was punished again? I didn't want to be another statistic.

This was exactly why I'd gone to school. This was exactly why I'd wanted to start my organization, to give omegas options, to give them a chance to live the life they wanted, the life *they* chose.

Instead, I had become a stereotype.

Violet. I could text Violet. Tell her I needed help. But then I would have to immediately erase the text. And what if she responded when one of the others were nearby? Would they read the text? Question me?

Punish me when they discovered I was trying to find a way out of this situation?

A dinner party. I could request a dinner party and invite Violet and her alphas. They would see…

They wouldn't see shit. Because I would be made up like the dutiful omega. Any evidence of abuse would be invisible to their eyes.

But maybe I could feel normal for a night. Violet and I were both omegas. It might be tense with a house full of alphas with two omegas, but if I behaved accordingly, they might release their tight grip on the reins a little, let me out of the house unchaperoned. And if we had some time alone, I could tell her what was happening, ask her to contact ORE for help…

Contact Kai.

Was this all nothing more than a pipedream? Another fantasy? I wanted out, but would I be given any choices if I was able to escape this prison? Would my family give a single fuck that one of my alphas had threatened me, had laid hands on me, had left bruises on me?

No. My fathers wouldn't. My mother was numb to the world around her.

My options were to accept this life and learn to be who they wanted me to be, or learn to live as an omega in a world that offered nothing but danger to my designation. A world who saw us as tools, vessels, prizes to be claimed.

I was still pacing when the garage door rumbled up, heralding the arrival of my alphas, and my anxiety spiked.

Standing in the living room with my hands fidgeting over my hair, smoothing it into place, then ensuring there were no wrinkles in my slacks and straightening my sweater, I watched and waited with a forced smile as my prospective pack came strolling through the door.

Each of them smiled as they passed, pressing quick kisses to my cheek. Even Anton hesitated to brush a hand over my hair and press his lips to my cheek and then lips as though nothing had transpired this morning.

They retreated to their rooms, and I was left standing there, unsure of what to do.

Kai had bent me over the arm of the couch and paddled my ass when I'd sassed him, when I'd slapped him. And then I'd climbed him like a tree and rode him until we were both crying out and exhausted.

The last thing I wanted was for any of the four alphas to touch me. My skin tingled where they'd kissed me, and not in a good way. The urge to reach up and scrub at the spot, to wipe their kisses away was overwhelming, but I resisted. Barely.

Eventually, the men joined me in the living room and Bryan placed a hand on the small of my back, guiding me into the dining room for dinner.

The men talked about business, leaving me out of the conversation, never bothering to ask about my day.

That attitude that I'd clung to my whole life tried to rear up, but I tamped it down, reminding myself of the throb still persistent in my cheek.

When there was a lull, I dabbed at my mouth with the cloth napkin and cleared my throat. "I was thinking...could we have a dinner party? I have a friend, Violet. She's an omega and newly mated, too. I thought it would be nice for our packs to meet. And for me to have a friend. An *omega* friend," I said, emphasizing the fact Violet was not a threat.

They consulted each other silently, raising their brows.

"What line of business is the pack in?" Chris asked.

"Um...I believe they're members of Omega Rescue and Extraction. Violet was one of the omegas they had rescued."

Deep chuckles erupted around the table. "Capitalized on her vulnerable state. Smart alphas. Moldable omega."

I bit the inside of my cheek to keep from cursing them. Those alphas didn't capitalize on a vulnerable omega. They had fallen hard for her. They treated her like a queen. They doted on her. They loved her. And, from the conversation we'd had, she adored all four of her alphas.

But I didn't say any of that. If it meant I could see faces other than this pack, I would let them believe anything they wanted.

"When would you want to have this dinner party?" Anton asked.

More and more, I was beginning to see that he was the head of this pack, even if all four were alphas, as well.

"I was thinking before the bonding ceremony." I batted my lashes at him. "I figured we might be a little too busy to entertain after that."

A sly grin stretched across his face as he reached his hand across the table and waited for me to place mine in it. He squeezed my fingers lightly, then brought them to his lips for a kiss. Day and night. Dr. Jekyll and Mr. fucking Hyde.

"You plan it and we'll be here. I would be honored to meet this omega friend of yours. Especially if she's half as beautiful as you."

A sick feeling twisted up in my gut, as though he was eluding that he would love the idea of adding a second omega to the pack.

That was damned near unheard of. An omega was to be cherished. Not only had these four proven they had no plans of giving me such a life, but they sure as hell couldn't spoil two omegas.

"Thank you. I promise it'll be perfect."

Anton's eyes traced my face, then lowered to my chest. I'd chosen a more conservative sweater today, especially after Eric's appearance in my bedroom the day he'd caught me napping. I was doing everything I could to keep them off of me as long as possible.

Because the day would come when my body would belong to them.

Worse, the day would come when my heat made me delirious and would convince my brain I wanted them. I dreaded that day with every breath in my lungs.

Kai

STORMING from the commander's office, I barely resisted the urge to slam his office door behind me.

Still no team. Still fucking displaced. Oh, but don't worry, he was going to find another assignment for me soon.

I wanted to be in the field. I wanted to be face to face with the evil fucks who preyed on omegas, on women, on anyone smaller or weaker than them.

I needed a fucking distraction.

It had been less than a month since the last time I'd seen Sophie's face, the last time I'd heard her voice. And time sure as hell hadn't made things any better. The whole *time healed all wounds* bull shit couldn't have been further from the truth.

It didn't help that I'd done my best to keep my distance from her when I'd noticed my growing attraction. It didn't help that I'd wasted precious time I could have had with her.

And it didn't help that I'd never uttered the words that had stayed on my tongue since the moment we'd finally given in to the feelings that had grown against our own wills.

I could have asked her to be with me. I could have promised to protect her, to provide for her. No. I could never buy her a mansion. I would never be able to supply her with fancy clothes and shoes and all that shit. But she appeared just as happy when we sat around the house in nothing but sweats and tees. She'd behaved more like herself when her hair was twisted into a knot, when her clothes swallowed her beautiful body, the oversized sweatshirts and sweaters hiding her perky tits.

All I could do now was hope and pray that she was happy. That was all I wanted for her. I'd known the moment I'd given in to my heart's desires that I would be ripping pieces of my heart away for her to take with her. I'd known my soul would be ripped in half the moment she walked out of my life. And as badly as it hurt, I would have done it all again. As long as I'd had that time with her, no matter how short it had been.

"You look happy," Wilder said as I passed his desk.

I grunted in response.

"Hey!" he called out.

I hesitated and glanced at him over my shoulder.

"Call Andrei. He said he has something to discuss with you."

Hope and dread pooled in my stomach. Hope that maybe there

was something I could finally do to keep from wallowing in my little one-bedroom cabin, going to bed alone every night, dreaming of Sophie's face.

Dread that Violet had received the code word, that she'd reached out for help.

There wasn't a fucking thing anyone could do to stop me if Sophie was in danger. I would personally drive my SUV through the front door to get to her, to drag her from that place. And then, I would never let her go. I'd get two more fucking jobs if that was what it took to give her the life she wanted, to keep her in the luxury she'd grown up in.

"What's up?" I asked.

Wilder's shoulders rose and fell. "Didn't tell me. Just told me to have you call him if I saw you today."

"He has my number."

"And you haven't been answering," Wilder said as he turned back to his computer.

I glared at the back of the beta's head for a second, but he wasn't lying. I'd been avoiding all phone calls, worried they would pull the whole *how ya holdin' up* shit. And I didn't want to talk about it with anyone. I didn't even want to think about how the hell I was holding up, or how my heart literally ached every moment of every day.

Waiting until I was in my SUV, I pulled the phone from my pocket and connected it to my Bluetooth, then touched Andrei's name on one of the many missed calls. The cab filled with ringing before the alpha's deep voice rumbled over the line.

"Well, shit. You *are* still alive," he said as an answer.

"Wilder said you needed to talk."

"Hey, Kai," Violet's sweet voice called over the line.

"Am I on speaker?"

"Yep," Liam answered.

Rolling my eyes, I dragged a hand down my race. "So what's up?"

"We've been invited to a dinner party," Violet said.

I swallowed back the growl. The woman didn't deserve my ire. "That's...uh, great."

"Keep listening," Liam said.

"*Sophie* invited us to a dinner party," Violet said, an obvious smile in her voice.

At the mere mention of her name, my heart kicked into gear until it raced behind my ribs.

"Yeah?"

"And I was thinking – she said to bring my pack."

And then I waited for her to continue. And waited some more.

"She's trying to say you should come with us," Chase said.

"I'm not pack."

"They don't know that," Violet said. "You can check on her, see with your own eyes that she's happy. She can see you. Maybe…I don't know. Maybe you two can have some closure."

"Or run off together into the sunset. I can have some horses delivered if you want to – Ow! Damn it, Andrei."

I could see Sophie's face again. I could see with my own eyes that she was being taken care of. I could see that she was happy and living the life she deserved. Then I could move on.

"Do they know how many are in your pack?" I asked.

"Unless Sophie told them, no," Violet answered.

"I won't smell like pack," I said.

"If you're asking for a cuddle, just say so," Liam said.

I smiled despite myself. He was an idiot. He never seemed to take anything serious and even looked like he was having fun on missions. But I knew how fierce he was in a fight. He was loyal to his team, his pack, his coworkers, and his omega.

"Dumbass," I said, not bothering to hide the chuckle in my voice. "When is this supposed to happen?"

"Tonight. Seven. At the pack's house," Andrei said.

"Your pack or hers?"

"Hers," Violet answered.

If her alphas got close enough, they would know I wasn't part of Violet's harem. I wouldn't smell like pack. But I didn't plan on cozying up with any of them, either. I'd spent more than enough time with them when I guarded Sophie during their short period of courtship.

"One more thing," Mac said, speaking for the first time since we'd started the call. "The bonding ceremony is in two weeks."

If my heart was racing before, it nearly skid to a complete stop at his words.

The bonding ceremony. They would put on a public display so the world would know they'd claimed an omega. Then, they would sink their teeth – and dicks – into the woman who'd crushed my heart in her petite little hands.

"I think you should go," Mac said in his gruff tone.

I was nodding before I realized no one could see me. "I'll meet you at your house."

"You should probably cuddle with one of us," Liam said. "I call dibs on the big boy."

"For fuck's sake," Andrei said, and I could almost picture him dragging a hand down his face. "I'll text you our address. Be here at six-thirty."

"Yep. See you then."

Shit. Dinner party in a fancy house. I would have to wear the same suit I wore on protection duties, the same suit I wore to that fancy ass restaurant where Sophie had first met her pack.

Not her pack. Not yet. They hadn't finalized anything. At least I hoped they hadn't.

Not that I had a say in shit. It was her life. She'd chosen…in a way. Out of the packs she'd met, they'd been the pack she'd chosen.

And, if she was happy, if she was being cherished the way I wished I could cherish her, then I would walk away and let her go.

My heart, however, would never be fully intact again.

CHAPTER 15

Sophie

This was probably the tenth time I'd checked the place settings around the table. I was sure I'd checked my hair, makeup, and outfit at least a dozen times. Not that Violet or her pack would give a shit about how I looked or whether or not I'd set out the perfect plates, glasses, and silverware.

But my alphas did. I was being judged by my soon-to-be pack on how well I entertained. After I'd suggested the dinner party, I had almost immediately regretted it. They had micromanaged everything, criticized my meal choices, *tsked* when I'd started pulling our regular dinnerware from the cabinets.

They wanted to see how well I entertained before they brought their high-profile friends around me, before they dragged me into public, before they invited hundreds of people to our bonding ceremony and ended up embarrassed.

Stopping by a mirror, I turned my cheek toward the light and frowned. The swelling from my most recent punishment had mostly gone down, but I'd had to use concealer to cover the fading green and yellow bruise.

I didn't bother with the bruises that covered my biceps and shoulders since they would be hidden by my cream-colored cashmere sweater. I didn't bother with those on my thighs when Anton had gripped me hard enough to leave dark bruises when I'd told him the same I'd told Eric, that I wanted to wait until the bonding ceremony. He'd held me in place while he'd masturbated, leaving his scent on my skin and demanding I still smell like him when he came home from work.

No matter how hard I fought, I was slowly being splintered apart, the woman I was being stolen from me, beaten out of me. I was allowing these alphas to train me, to mold me into what they wanted.

I hated myself. I hated to see my reflection in the mirror, unfamiliar with the soulless eyes looking back at me.

Ashamed. I was ashamed of allowing myself to be broken the same way my mother had been broken, the same way my sister and brother had been broken. Ashamed that I'd given up on my plans of building something to keep omegas safe, to keep us from a life exactly like the one I was currently living.

Ashamed that I'd walked away from the only man I had every truly loved because I followed the rules set forth by my family. I should have told them all to go to hell. I should have clung to Kai, told him I didn't need a pack, a big house, or pretty jewelry.

I just wanted him.

But it was too late. The trajectory of my life was moving faster than I could process. All I could do was hold on and hope I didn't completely lose myself.

"Looks great," Chris said as he entered the room.

The three alphas were polite to me, if not slightly aloof at times. Only Anton had manhandled me and downright abused me since I'd dared to defy him that first time. Even when I kept my mouth shut and tried to be agreeable or behave the way he expected, he found one reason or another to grab onto my arm too tightly, squeeze my shoulder too hard, or to shove me onto the couch when he felt I was taking too long to cuddle with my pack.

And to think I'd found his scent most appealing in the beginning. To think it was Eric who'd scared me, who I had thought would be the one I would have to worry about forcing himself on me once I was in their house.

"Thank you," I said, tilting my head when he leaned in for a peck to my cheek before running his nose along my throat.

"Good omega," he said when he realized I'd used scent blockers.

I hadn't done it for him. I had done it in hopes of keeping the possessive urges of so many alphas from boiling over and completely ruining the night and any hope of seeing Violet – or freedom – again.

"You look beautiful," Bryan said as he passed, running a gentle hand over the top of my head like I was a fucking dog.

"Thank you, alpha," I said.

Another thing I'd learned was that the men preferred I use their title as much as possible.

Eric cupped my cheek and pressed a soft kiss to my lips. "Everything looks perfect. Maybe you should help the coordinator plan the ceremony. You have a natural eye for entertaining."

For most omegas, that would have been a compliment. Hell, for most women that might have been a compliment. But I hadn't busted my ass in college for my degree to plan parties.

I smiled sweetly, keeping the softness in my face as we waited for our guests, even if every muscle in my body was tense.

Minutes now. Any minute, Violet and her pack would pull into the driveway and step into the house. My house. Our house.

Nerves tickled my belly and I laid a hand over it.

Eric's gaze dipped and then raised to my face, his eyes narrowing. "Are you sick?"

I plastered that damn smile on my face again. "Just nervous. This is my very first dinner party I planned on my own. I just want everything to be perfect."

"It will be." He pressed another soft kiss to my lips, and I swallowed hard, fighting the urge to pull away.

. . .

Kai

As much as I'd hoped he'd been joking, I'd been so fucking wrong. Liam was practically draped over my lap, a shit eating grin wide on his face. Violet sat on my other side, both her arms wrapped around my bicep as she periodically rubbed her cheek along my shoulder, resulting in the cab of the vehicle being filled with long, rumbling growls.

It didn't matter that the alphas knew I didn't want their omega. It was a natural possessive urge to protect Violet from other alphas.

They were ensuring I smelled like pack so there would be no questions when I stepped through the door with them. Hopefully, I had stayed in the background enough when they'd started courting Sophie that they wouldn't remember me. Or at least they would think I was her guard *and also* a member of Violet's pack, another of her alphas.

We were basing a whole lot of shit on speculation.

My only goal was to see Sophie, to see for myself that I hadn't made a mistake by letting her move in with these rich fuckers, that she was happy and living an omega's dream.

Andrei was behind the wheel with Mac riding shotgun. Liam still draped himself over my left side, Violet on my right. Chase was enjoying himself far too much in the third row, chuckling periodically when Liam would bob his head, pretending to give me a blowjob.

I didn't bother saying shit. It would only encourage him, especially if he was getting a laugh from his mates.

A low whistle pulled my attention to the windshield and halted Liam's shenanigans.

I'd forgotten this pack had yet to see the mini mansion where Sophie now lived.

"Wow," Violet said. "It's bigger than our house."

"Do you want a bigger house?" Chase asked from the last row of seats.

Violet tilted her head up to me and rolled her eyes. "No, baby. I don't want a bigger house. I was simply stating a fact."

"We should get a fence like this," Liam said as Andrei hit the call button and waited for the gate to swing open and allow the SUV through.

I felt as though I was vibrating as the vehicle crept toward the house. I stared straight ahead, watching shadows move across the windows. The entire house was lit up and ready for company, ready for a fancy dinner party.

At least everyone was dressed the part. Part of me was looking forward to seeing how Liam would behave around these guys; the fucker rarely kept his thoughts to himself.

Andrei would stand out even in his suit. The tattoos that covered his body peeked above the collar of his button-up and along the backs of his hands and fingers. He hadn't bothered to remove any of the jewelry that decorated his ears or nose. He was the complete opposite of the strait-laced, uptight fuckers who'd won Sophie's hand.

"You sure you're ready for this?" Mac asked from the front seat, looking at me over his shoulder.

I nodded, but kept my eyes on the front door, waiting to get a glimpse of Sophie. I wasn't sure whether it was a good idea, but I was ready. Even if I had to make an excuse to leave the table and step outside. One more look. I wanted to see for myself that she was safe and happy. That she was living the life of an omega's dreams.

"Chase," Andrei said.

"Yeah."

"When we get out, sniff Kai but make it inconspicuous. Make sure he smells like pack."

"If you want to drive around the neighborhood a couple times, I can make sure he's covered in my—"

"Don't you dare even say it," Chase said with a chuckle and a growl.

Liam was nothing more than a flirt. He liked to play games. While

I knew exactly what he was going to say, it had been in an effort to lighten the mood. And, as much as I hated to admit it, it had worked. I felt my lips quirk at the corners as I jabbed my elbow into his side.

Chase leaned over the pack seat and gave a quick sniff. "He's good. I smell Violet and Liam. A little of each of us, too."

But would it be enough to convince the alphas inside I was simply joining *my* pack for a dinner where we'd been invited?

The front door opened and a tall shadow filled the space.

"Show time," Andrei said, killing the engine and pushing from his seat.

He opened the door for Violet and brought her hand to his lips before tucking it into the crook of his elbow. I scooted and followed her out and tensed when she looped her other arm through my elbow, as well.

A soft growl trickled from Andrei but was quickly cut off when Violet squeezed his bicep hard. "Don't screw this up," she whispered softly without moving her lips.

Mac, Liam, and Chase led the way to the porch, then shook hands with the alpha I had nearly beat to a pulp weeks ago. Eric. This was the fucker who'd nearly gone into rut with Sophie, trapping her in the bathroom and pawing at her.

Clenching my teeth, I swallowed back the growl as the memory slammed into my brain, playing vividly behind my lids every time I blinked.

"We should have brought Wilder," Violet whispered just before the three of us made it to the porch.

As a beta, Wilder's presence might have kept me calm. Or he might have been invisible to me, another barrier between myself and Sophie.

"Thank you for joining us," Eric said, shaking each alpha's hand as we approached but simply dipping his head in Violet's direction.

"I'm so happy to meet Sophie's pack. I'm Violet. The three beauties over there are Liam, Chase, and Mac. And these two hunks are Andrei and Kai."

Eric's eyes brushed over each of us before they landed on me. He nodded, then did a quick double take. For some reason, I'd hoped these rich fucks hadn't bothered taking much notice of me. But after nearly throwing Eric across the room, it was obvious my face was burned into his memory.

"It's wonderful to meet you all. Come on in," he said. The smile was still there on his lips, but it didn't reach his eyes and he was now tense as he stepped through the front door and onto the marble floored foyer.

Yep. Just as fancy and pretentious as I remembered.

The difference this time was Sophie's sweet scent filled the space, nearly covering the aroma of whatever meal that had been prepared.

Three more alphas stepped forward. When the man in front, Bryan, stepped to the side, my Sophie was revealed, Anton's arm around her shoulders.

Her eyes widened, her lips parted, and I struggled the urge to rush forward, rip Anton's arm from his body, then carry her from this house so I could sequester her away and fuck her until neither of us could move. Then latch my teeth onto her shoulder and mark her as mine forever.

"Mr. Janse," Anton greeted me.

"Kai," I said.

"I'm surprised to see you again. I had no idea you were a member of Violet's pack."

Violet tilted her head back and beamed up at me. I forced a smile on my face and winked down at her.

When my attention returned to Sophie, she looked tense. Anton's hand was on her shoulder, and I could have sworn I saw her wince slightly. But there was a smile on her face, albeit as forced as my own. It didn't make her eyes shine or twinkle the way they did when she was truly happy.

"You have a beautiful home," Violet said, filling the silence as eight alphas sized each other up.

This had been a bad idea. It was going to be hard enough being around Sophie when I couldn't touch her, when she smelled of her new alphas, but the room was now filled with possessive alphas and two omegas.

The next few hours could be tense. Hell, they could turn dangerous.

But I couldn't control the actions of the others. I had come here for one reason and so far, I wasn't convinced Sophie was in the best pack for her. She looked…tired. Her eyes weren't filled with that fire I'd grown to adore. And, I might have imagined it, but her left cheek looked a touch swollen.

Her hair was down, but as far as I could see, there were no silvery crescents on her neck indicating they'd marked her yet. They would want a public display of a bonding ceremony. Then they would make it official, complete with a newspaper article of their most recent conquest, their prized possession officially and legally owned.

"Thank you. We try," Bryan said. "Please. Come sit. We weren't sure whether you would prefer red or white wine, so we've made sure we had a good selection on hand."

"Beer?" Liam said, causing Chase to huff a surprised laugh he tried – and failed – to cover with a cough.

"I think I can wrangle up a beer or two," Bryan said with a wink at Liam.

Wait…was that a teasing wink or a flirt?

And why the fuck did I care? There was an alpha holding my omega in place with a hand on her shoulder. She didn't move forward to hug Violet, didn't make eye contact with anyone including me. It was as though she was seeing through us while keeping that fake ass smile plastered on her pretty lips.

The group surged forward, following Bryan's lead.

But not Anton and Sophie. Anton's eyes were boring holes into the side of my head until I turned my attention to him.

Violet tugged my arm, keeping me glued to her side, and forced me forward until we were standing in an opulent dining room, the same room where I had watched over Sophie when she'd begun to court this pack. The table was bigger now, more chairs pushed up to the table.

Andrei pulled out a chair and seated Violet, then looked pointedly at me then at the chair to her right.

Anton stepped into the room behind all of us, seating Sophie on his left elbow before taking the chair at the head of the table while Bryan took the chair at the foot. Mac sat beside Sophie, leaving a chair between them. Liam, and Chase sat on his other side.

Sophie didn't look at me. Or wouldn't. She would raise her eyes when others spoke, nodded or answered if anyone addressed her directly. But she didn't lead the conversation, didn't offer any topics.

She sat ramrod straight at the table, her eyes constantly darting to Anton as though checking in with him.

This didn't seem like a happy pack. Sophie didn't look like a happy, cherished, and spoiled omega. She looked…scared.

And every cell in my fucking body was on fire with the need to rescue her as I had so many omegas through the years.

That wasn't my decision to make. Her family hadn't asked us for help, hadn't called ORE to extract their daughter from a dangerous situation. And, although she looked closed off, she didn't appear to have suffered physically at the hands of her new pack.

But if I'd learned anything during my years on this planet it was that sometimes the emotional and verbal abuse left deeper scars than physical kind.

CHAPTER 16

Sophie

nton sat me on his left side strategically – he was right-handed. This way, he could keep the nearly painful grip on my knee under the table, reminding me where I belonged, reminding me that he knew about Kai and me, while eating and behaving as though everything was fine.

And reminding me he was fully aware that Kai was not a member of Violet's pack.

What was he doing here? A new wave of shame washed over me when I'd looked into his beautiful blue eyes. My heart swelled and began to race, and I had tensed, ready to throw myself into his arms. Until Anton's thumb dug into the muscle of my shoulder, stilling any movement, any thought. There would be another bruise there by tomorrow. Probably on my knee, as well.

It seemed it didn't matter what I did; Anton was going to do every-thing in his power to keep me in my place and remind me I was his property.

So, I'd kept my eyes off of Kai. In fact, I was afraid to look any of them in the eye, equally terrified I'd be punished later and terrified they would see through the mask I was struggling to keep in place.

At least I didn't have to choke down much food. Anton was watching every bite I ate and fixed my plate himself, ensuring I didn't overeat. I would be surprised if I had a chance to enjoy the cheesecake the staff had prepared for dessert.

"More wine, my sweet omega?" Anton asked, finally releasing my knee to lift the bottle and top off my glass.

"Thank you, alpha," I said, forcing the words through my closing throat.

I didn't need to look up to know Kai was watching me closely, waiting for any sign that he needed to step in, to protect me as he had for weeks.

I was no longer his responsibility. He was no longer paid by my family to act as private security for their prized omega daughter.

When Anton finished pouring more Merlot into my glass, I nearly sagged with relief when he didn't return his hand to my knee to punish the joint and skin there further.

The others were fully aware of how Anton treated me, yet they did nothing to step in and stop him. They simply took turns pawing at me, forcing me to strip so they could leave their release, their scent on my bare skin.

But I'd gone this far without any of them entering me, without any of the four knotting me. I supposed I should count myself blessed, especially knowing how much worse so many omegas had it around the world.

Dinner was delicious and the packs appeared to get along, even if the lines of conversation were benign and closer to small talk than any effort to bond or truly get to know each other.

As the plates began to clear, I smiled over to Anton. "Should I get the dessert?"

He reached over and took my hand, bringing his fingers to my lips for a kiss as though he was an affectionate and doting alpha. "I'll give you a hand."

Anton stood and pulled my chair out, taking my hand and looping it through his elbow before leading me from the dining room and into the kitchen.

The dessert plates were already on the table. I didn't exactly need help carrying a platter of cheesecake from one room to another.

Which meant Anton wasn't happy with something I had done.

Releasing my hand, he stalked toward me, backing me across the kitchen until my hips hit the counter and he loomed over me.

"What the fuck is he doing here?" he growled softly enough the others wouldn't hear him.

"I don't know," I answered. Because I didn't. I truly believed he would forever remain as nothing more than a memory.

And that beautifully rugged face had appeared and the tiniest sliver of ice had begun to melt in my heart.

He ran his nose along my neck. "Do I need to remind you where you belong?"

"No, alpha," I squeaked out.

I hated this life. I hated myself. I hated who I'd become. Who I'd allowed them to turn me into.

His hands landed on the counter on either side of me, trapping me, caging me. "I don't think I'll wait for the ceremony. I think tonight I'll remind you of where you belong. I'll have you begging for release, then begging me to stop. After I've knotted you a few times, after I've had my fill, I'll make sure your other alphas consummate our union. I'm going to dark bond you and make you my sweet little omega, have you begging on all fours every night."

He stepped back and straightened his clothes.

"If I catch you saying one word to that alpha, you will regret it. I promise you that."

He grabbed the platter and left the room as I struggled to suck air into my lungs and control the shaking throughout my body.

Tonight. Anton was going to force himself on me tonight. I no longer had any say. I had tried for coy, demure, tried to pretend I wanted this fairy tale romance of the five of us waiting until we were bonded.

Anton was going to use my body as punishment.

Tears burned the backs of my eyes and clogged my throat. I had to get my emotions under control before leaving the kitchen. Violet and her pack didn't know me well, but Kai did. He would know instantly if something was wrong. Hell, they would all smell the change in my scent, even with the blockers I'd used while bathing.

Focusing all my energy, I shoved every emotion deep, forced the memories of Kai into a box deep inside and locked it tight, then squared my shoulders. I glanced at myself in the reflection of the window over the sink. Makeup perfect. Hair perfect. Clothes perfect.

I was the image of omega royalty.

Squaring my shoulders, I schooled my face into a soft smile and returned to the dining room. Kai's eyes immediately found mine, but I didn't so much as acknowledge his presence. I wouldn't. I'd already been warned.

Anton knew Kai wasn't one of Violet's alphas. He knew the two of us had shared time together, shared a bed. He'd scented him on me even though we had both tried to cover our tracks.

The tension in the air was palpable even as everyone sliced into their servings of dessert.

"Aren't you going to have any?" Violet asked.

A hand landed on my knee and squeezed until I swore I saw stars. Biting back the grunt of pain, I smiled and shook my head. "I'm not a big fan of cheesecake."

Lie. Total lie. It was probably my favorite dessert.

"You are missing out, girl," Violet said as she slid a bite between her lips.

"This is delicious," Liam said. He pointed a fork in my direction. "Did you make it?"

"No," I said with a shake of my head.

Liam waited, watching, his brows raised. "Hey, Anton?"

Anton raised his brows toward Liam.

"How about you release your grip on Sophie there and let her answer a fucking question?"

Growls erupted around the table, the loudest coming from Kai.

Alphas rose, chairs toppled. Violet was pulled from the table and shoved behind Mac's body.

"I think it's time for you all to leave," Anton ordered.

"Sophie," Kai said.

I averted my eyes as I saw Anton look at me from the corner of my eye.

"Sophie, look at me," he barked.

Well, shit. The force of his alpha caused my body to react before I had a chance to stop it.

Turning my eyes to his, I bit my lip to keep it from quivering.

"Is he hurting you? Are they hurting you?"

"It's time to go. All of you. You're no longer welcome in my home," Anton said, throwing his napkin on his plate and stepping toward the entry to the dining room as though he figured everyone would obey and follow.

"Sophie?" Violet's soft voice broke through the cacophony of snarls and growls. "Do you need help?"

I pushed to my feet slowly, my eyes bouncing from Violet to each of her alphas, before finally settling on Kai.

Anton returned to my side, his arm wrapped around my shoulders, his hand resting near my neck. To an outsider, it looked as though he was simply protecting his omega or even holding her.

What the room didn't see was the way his thumb was shoved deep into the muscle there, hard enough that I could no longer bite back the whimper.

It felt like slow motion when I turned to look into Anton's face, turned to Kai, and opened my mouth.

"Evergreen," I said softly.

Kai

ONE WORD. That was all it took for the world to completely shift onto its head.

I rounded the table too fast for anyone to stop me and ripped Anton away from Sophie.

Unfortunately, it caused her to lose her balance and topple to the table, her hands slapping on the surface before she could fall over.

"Get her out of here," Mac said. I didn't know who he was talking to and I didn't give a fuck.

Evergreen. Her code word. *Our* code word. She was telling me it was time for her to go, that she needed an out.

Liam had brought to everyone's attention that Anton was controlling Sophie's actions with a tight grip on her knee under the table. He'd had a better angle than me. When Anton had gripped her shoulder as though to hold her close, I'd seen the tightness in her eyes, the wince on her face a second before she whimpered in pain.

He'd been hurting her to keep her under his control. Right in front of us. In front of me.

Had the other three had any part in the emptiness I saw in my beautiful omega's eyes, in the way she moved and behaved as though her spirit had been completely broken?

I didn't give Anton time to climb to his feet before I was on him, my fists swinging and making contact with any part of his body I could reach. Blood ran from his nose, his mouth, a cut that opened on his cheek as I continued to pummel him.

Hands gripped at me, tried to pull me free. With a roar of rage, I shook them loose and continued to unleash my fury on the man who'd dared to hurt my sweet Sophie, who'd taken her away from me with promises of paradise and given her nothing but hell.

"Stop!" Sophie screamed over the chaos, over the cursing of the other members of this pack, over Violet's alphas attempting to escort the omegas from the room while keeping the fight fair.

"Please, Kai. Stop! He's not worth it!"

"Get her out of here," Mac yelled.

Hands gripped me and pulled me away, familiar scents wrapping around me and keeping me from swinging on the people who'd given me a chance to not only see Sophie again, but to rescue her from a fucked up situation.

"He's done, brother. Enough," Andrei said, wrapping his arms around my chest like a vise and pulling me from a bloodied, coughing Anton.

"She's mine," he said through bloodied, split lips. "Her father sold her to me. She's mine."

Not ours. He hadn't said she was ours, as in a member of the pack. But the others had touched her as they'd passed her, brushed their fingers over her shoulder or through her hair as though claiming her with their scent.

"We gotta go," Andrei said.

"I'll call the police. You'll all be arrested for kidnapping and lose your fucking jobs."

Andrei released me long enough to hover over Anton. "You do that. You tell the police that members of ORE entered a house where they found an omega in clear distress. You tell them that we witnessed possible abuse and extricated the woman who alerted her *true* alpha that she was in danger."

Her true alpha. Me. *I* was her fucking alpha. She was *my* fucking omega.

Violet and Sophie stood near the entry to the dining room with Liam and Chase blocking them from the three other alphas who stared on with wide eyes.

"Did you know?" I growled out, my attention bouncing from one to the other. "Did you know he was hurting her?"

Their silence was all I needed to know.

Stalking forward, I was prepared to dole out the same punishment on them as I had on Anton. They hadn't bothered to protect her. They hadn't stopped their pack leader from hurting a woman half their size.

"No, brother. It's time to go," Mac said, stepping in my way and blocking me with his big body.

He wasn't as tall as me, but as broad and I wondered if I could knock him down to get to the other three alphas.

"It's not worth it," Sophie said, her sweet voice snapping me out of my rage. "Take me home."

Turning so fast I almost lost my balance, I closed the space between us, lifted her in my arms, and carried her from the dining room, through the living room, and out of the house, her face pressed to my neck as I inhaled her essence as deep into my lungs as possible, the scent I feared I would never experience again.

Violet, Liam, and Chase hurried out behind us with Mac and Andrei taking up the rear, watching all of our backs.

"There's room in the third row," Chase offered, opening the door for me and waiting for me to climb in with Sophie cradled to my chest.

Violet, Liam, and Chase took the second row. Mac and Andrei reclaimed their places up front.

"I should have never let you go," I said into Sophie's hair, tears burning my eyes as my chest squeezed and my heart broke all over again.

"I never thought I would see you again," she said, her voice muffled against my neck.

I kissed the top of her head, her temple, anywhere I could reach in this position.

Alone. I needed to be alone with her. I needed to touch her, to hold her, to feel her below my hands, below my body.

I needed to mark her as mine.

But first, we had a few things to discuss. I didn't have a pack for her. I didn't have the numbers to keep her safe the way Violet's pack protected her. I would shield her with my own body, give her any and everything she could ever want from me. But she needed to know that turning her back on that pack meant turning her back on her family.

It meant living in a one-bedroom, one-bathroom place with only me. If she wanted to add to our pack in the future, I wouldn't stop her.

But for now, I wanted to spend nothing short of a week devoting every second to erasing their scent from her, to helping her get that fire back in her eyes, to finding the fight and strength I'd seen from the first day I'd met her.

CHAPTER 17

Kai

My vehicle was still at Andrei's house, but I didn't want to waste the time to retrieve it before taking Sophie back to my place.

It was a far cry from the palace where she'd been living, but it was safe. It was mine. It was *ours*.

I prayed the way she was clinging to me, her statement that she should have never left my side meant we were together. But, if she decided she wanted the security of a larger pack, I would once again let her go. And the last slivers that were left of my heart would go with her.

The second the SUV pulled to a stop outside my tiny cabin, I was damned near kicking at the door to get it open. Liam pulled it open and ran ahead of me, concern and confusion on his face.

"She in danger, man? Do we need to keep guard?"

"What?"

Liam's eyes darted around the yard, and I realized Chase and Mac had followed me, as well.

"Fuck. No. I just…" I looked down at Sophie.

Realization dawned on the men's faces.

"My keys are in my pocket," I said, twisting so someone could dig them out.

I could have easily set Sophie on her feet and opened the door myself, but I had no desire to release her, and her arms had a choke-hold around my neck.

Liam dug into my front pocket, grazing the side of my cock.

"Dude," I said, glaring at him over Sophie's head.

"What?"

Fucker. I knew he had no interest in me, but the asshole had a mean streak and liked to bust balls.

Keys in hand, he flipped a few until he came to the one that was obviously a house key.

The door was barely opened before I kicked it in, carried Sophie over the threshold, then kicked it closed behind me.

As I rushed through the house, I heard the door open, heard my keys hit the floor inside, then the door closed again.

I'd left the keys in the lock in my haste to get Sophie behind closed doors so I could check her over, so I could cover her in my scent, so I could erase the nightmare of her time with that pack from her memory.

Sitting on the edge of my bed, I tugged at Sophie, forcing her to look at me.

"Princess," I said softly.

I'd used that word as a jab in the beginning. And then she'd become royalty to me, the fucking queen of my life.

"Look at me, baby."

She pulled away, and my heart shattered all over again. Her face was tear streaked, her makeup smudged under her eyes.

The part that sent rage coursing through me was where her makeup had rubbed onto my shirt, revealing a healing bruise on her right cheek.

"What the fuck," I growled, reaching up to gently grasp her chin and turn her face so I could get a better look.

Her lips quivered as more tears welled and trailed down her cheeks. "I should have never left you," she squeaked out, her voice full of so many emotions that my own eyes welled with tears.

"I should have never let you go. I should have begged you to stay with me. I should have…fuck, I don't know. Gotten six more jobs so I could be the kind of man your fathers would approve."

"Fuck my fathers. This is their fault." She swiped at her face angrily. "*My* fault."

"Nope. Not doing that."

I leaned in and feathered a soft kiss to her lips. A growl rattled up my chest and through my parted lips.

"You smell like him. Like them."

Of course she did. I'd watched as Anton and the others had touched her as often as possible the moment we'd stepped into the door as though scent marking her, proving to the room full of alphas that she was off limits.

Standing with her in my arms, I stepped into the bathroom and used my elbow to flip on the light. I sat her on the vanity only long enough to turn on the shower spray and waited for it to warm. I would stay in there with her, fully clothed if that was what she needed, until the evidence of her time at that house was completely erased from her skin.

But from the look in her eyes, it would take more than a shower to heal the wounds to her heart and mind.

Sophie slid off the vanity and turned to the mirror, staring at herself as though a stranger were looking back. Tears welled but she blinked them away. With shaking hands, she gripped the front of the soft, cream-colored sweater and slowly brought it to her nose, sniffing once.

With a scream of rage, she began yanking open the drawers of the vanity until she reached in and yanked out a pair of scissors.

"Sophie? Princess. What are you–"

She began to shred the sweater she wore, slicing through it until she could rip it from her body. Then, she reached for her waist length hair.

"Sweetheart–"

But I wasn't fast enough. She gripped the ends and began hacking away until the length barely grazed the tops of her shoulders.

Clumps of honey blonde wavy hair sat on the vanity top and in the sink. She rubbed her hands across her face as though trying to wipe the rest of the makeup off.

All I could do was stand there and watch, wait until she needed me, until she allowed me to help her.

While staring, my eyes wandered from her neck to her shoulders, down her back to her waist. So many fucking bruises. Smaller ones like fingers that had dug into her skin, like hands that had gripped her too hard. And that white hot rage returned.

"Sophie," I barked.

She stiffened and raised her eyes to my face in the mirror, suddenly appearing to remember she wasn't alone.

"Did they do that to you?"

Her body shook with a sob.

Turning to face me, she undid the button of her slacks and shoved them down her legs to reveal bruises marring her beautifully soft skin, speckled across her thighs and knees as though they'd…

"Did they touch you?" I asked, unable to keep the growl from my voice.

"I kept them from fucking me. But they made sure I stayed a good little omega while they covered me in their–" A sob cut off her words.

Rushing across the room, I hugged her to my chest and walked us to the shower, my clothes still in place, her bra and panties still covering her.

I wanted her under my hands but only when she was whole. Only when she remembered she could trust me. Only when any fear of alphas had been washed away permanently.

Sophie

. . .

KAI and I had stood under the shower spray - him fully dressed –
until the water began to run cool. He quickly washed me with
neutralizing, scent cancelling soap, apologizing as he removed my bra
and panties so he could make sure I was fully clean.

Once I was rinsed, he carried me from the stall and dried me with
a soft, fluffy towel as water *drip, drip, dripped* from his hair and soaked
clothing.

"You're wet," I said as a strange feeling of hysteria built in my chest.
It was so absurd, Kai fussing over drying me while his clothes clung
to him.

Giggles started and then I couldn't stop them. As he pulled his
shirt over his head then shucked his pants, the giggles turned to sobs.

He was fully naked when he gathered me into his arms and carried
me from the bathroom, past the bed, and into the living room. I would
have rather we laid under the blankets, skin against skin, but he
dropped onto the couch, practically stretching his entire length over
me while keeping the weight on his elbows.

"Does this help, or is it making it worse?" he asked, raising his head
to look into my face.

His presence was like a balm on a burn. And when his chest began
to vibrate with a purr, the tears and sobbing slowly ebbed.

"Please don't move," I begged, clinging to his shoulders and wrapping my legs around his waist to keep him in place.

I didn't care that I could feel his cock against my core. I didn't care
that we were completely naked on his couch.

All I cared about was the fact I was safe. I was in Kai's arms. We
were together.

I knew there would be repercussions. I knew the moment my
family discovered that I'd walked away from that pack, that Kai had
beat Anton to a pulp on my behalf, I would no longer have a family.

And I couldn't find a single fuck to give no matter how hard I
searched my heart.

Kai didn't rotate his hips, didn't nudge himself against me. His hands were behind my shoulder blades as he kept his weight on his elbows, and he held me as tightly as he could from this position.

His soft lips feathered across my forehead, my nose, my cheeks, my temples. I turned my head and caught his lips before he could retreat. We didn't deepen the kiss. I didn't push my tongue into his mouth. His hands didn't roam my body.

It was as though we were reassuring ourselves that this was real. He was grounding me with his warmth, with his strength.

With his love.

My eyes grew heavy as the tears dried on my cheeks.

"Are you super uncomfortable?" I asked.

"I'm fine. Am I hurting you?"

"No. Please don't move," I said as my eyes slowly closed and exhaustion swept me under.

When I woke, a sense of panic clawed at me and I began to struggle against the weight pinning me down. Until the scent of freshly baked cookies, of vanilla and sugar and warmth processed through my groggy mind.

Kai turned his head and peered at me, his brilliant blue eyes searching my face.

"You okay?"

"Is this real? Am I really here? Am I really free? With you?"

His body shook with a soft chuckle. "It's real. I'm real."

Kai rolled to the side, no longer pinning me, but kept an arm over my waist.

"Are you okay?" His eyes swept over my face and a hand lifted to toy with the uneven ends of my newly cut hair.

"Not yet. But I will be."

Shit. I had hacked my hair off last night. There had been this absurd urge to rid myself of any and all evidence of my time with the pack. And that included my perfectly curled and styled hair.

I was done being the good little omega. I was done being perfect. And I was done ignoring the swell of love I felt at the mere thought of Kai.

"I don't need a pack," I told him, turning to face him fully. "I don't need a big house. I don't need expensive crap. I just need you, Kai. And...I want to start my organization."

He nodded as I spoke. "Anything you need. I'll help in any way I can. I don't know anything about starting a business, but I'll help however you need."

Tears pricked the backs of my eyes again, but this time it was from a mixture of emotions.

"I'm so ashamed of myself," I admitted in a small voice.

Kai's hand was gentle as he pushed strands of hair off my forehead, then trailed the tips of his fingers down my cheek.

Anton, Chris, Bryan, and Eric had been what society saw as successful alphas, as well-dressed, well-raised gentlemen.

Kai was big and broody and muscular and had hidden tattoos, yet was so gentle and sweet and kind, even if he hid it behind a hard outer shell.

"My sweet marshmallow," I said through a smile.

"Did you just call me a marshmallow?"

"I meant to say something else but couldn't think of a better analogy. You're all hard and prickly on the outside, a hard outer shell. But you're soft and squishy and sweet on the inside."

"You're comparing me to candy," he said, pressing his lips into a line to keep from smiling.

Running a finger down the side of his face, I let my eyes trace the path then roamed every inch, memorizing the face I thought I would only ever see again in my dreams.

The smile faded from his face as his eyes focused on my shoulder where I knew there would be a bruise. His fingers touched the fading bruise on my cheek then softly prodded the marks where Anton's fingers had dug into my neck as a warning.

"I want to fucking kill him," he growled.

I simply nodded.

"Did the others hurt you?"

I wasn't sure if he remembered much from last night, when he'd bellowed at the others, asking if they'd hurt me, if they'd known

Anton was hurting me. He'd been in a rage and I had feared he would kill Anton then go to prison for the rest of his life.

"Not…not like Anton did." We were pressed together, almost lined chest to chest, thigh to thigh. "Some of the bruises on my thighs are from the others when they'd hold—"

I couldn't finish the sentence. Simply saying the words made the shame and disgust come rushing back until I felt as though I were drowning.

"We can report them," Kai said, his voice deep and growly as though he was hanging on to his anger by a thread. "Press charges. Make sure no other omega suffers at their hands."

My mouth popped open to say no, but I nodded. How could I say no and allow another omega to suffer? It was the complete opposite of what I wanted to do with my life, the plans I'd made before my fathers had forged a different path for me.

"Yeah," I said. "I think I want to do that. We should go today while the bruises are all fresh."

A victim. I was a victim. I'd come to the halfway house so full of strength and hope. I'd had this hope that I would find a pack who would respect me, who would love me and cherish me the way I did them.

Instead, I'd found a single alpha who made me feel as though not only did the world revolve around me but that I was capable of anything as long as he was by my side.

The thought of going into the police department and having my bruises photographed, having to write down all the incidences of abuse I'd suffered at the hands of Anton, having to possibly go to court and look him and the others in the eye sent anxiety burning through my veins.

"Hey," he said, gently turning my face so I had to look him in the eye. "I'll be right by your side the whole time. No one will ever hurt you again. I swear to you on my own fucking life. I will never leave your side again."

Pressing my hand against his, I held it to my cheek and smiled. "I trust you."

CHAPTER 18

Kai

While Sophie had showered and changed into a pair of clothes Violet had brought her, we'd all waited patiently, quietly, until she was ready to head into ORE. We didn't bother with going to the police department. It was my organization's job to keep omegas safe.

And I'd fucking failed her.

Violet sat beside her on the trip there, holding her hand while all five of us alphas drove her to headquarters. Violet sat with her while she'd filled out forms, while Sophie's bruises had been photographed, and when the commander had questioned her.

She'd also tapped on her phone a few times and I'd caught a sly smile on her face and wondered what she was up to.

By the time we were done, Sophie's eyes were swollen from crying, her nose and cheeks were pink, and she looked exhausted.

"Would you mind stopping by our house before you guys go home?" Violet asked, that same sly smile on her face.

"Sure," Sophie said, her voice sounding so tired.

I wanted to have her in my arms, behind closed doors alone.

The trip back to Violet's pack house wasn't far from headquarters, but Sophie's head leaned on my shoulder as her eyes drifted shut. She needed rest. She needed food and a nap.

There was a new vehicle in the driveway when Andrei pulled up. "What did you do, omega?" he asked, looking at his mate in the mirror. There was obvious affection on his rugged face.

"Oh, nothing."

She pushed from the door and waited for Sophie to climb free.

No one waited outside the house; the vehicle parked was empty. I was instantly on guard, but it was obvious Violet knew exactly who was inside the house.

She wrapped a hand around Sophie's and led her inside. Omegas tended to be possessive of their alphas around other omegas. But it was obvious these women weren't attracted to each other's alphas. And Violet had believed she was a beta until a short time before she'd met her pack.

I followed closely behind Sophie, wanting to pull her from Violet and wrap her up in my arms. But she leaned against Violet, seemed to enjoy the closeness of a friend after being separated from everyone for so long.

"What did you do?" Chase asked as he stepped into the living room first. "Hey, Devyn."

Violet and Sophie stepped in next with me on their heels. There was a beta in the kitchen, a salon chair positioned near the kitchen sink, and all kind of hair tools spread out on the counter.

"Your hair looks like crap. You need it fixed."

"Violet. For fuck's sake. I thought I lacked tact," Liam chuckled.

"My girl doesn't want to be coddled. She wants to be herself. And her hair is way too pretty for this hack job. Devyn is one of the best I've ever had."

"She means the best hairdresser who's ever done her hair," Chase said with a blush.

"Yeah. That. Not that he isn't gorgeous. Oh, and packless," she said, the last part almost as though she was trying to sneak it in without notice.

I bit back the growl as Devyn reached forward and ran his fingers through Sophie's hair, checking the length.

"It's not bad. You're beautiful regardless. But yeah, this haircut is a hack job. You definitely need a new stylist."

"*I* was the stylist. And I'm pretty sure those were beard scissors."

The room got quiet at that announcement. It wasn't my business to share hers. She'd had a moment, a point where she'd broken. She'd done everything she could to erase as much of that pack from her as possible. She'd cut her hair knowing it would no longer represent the perfection that had been expected of her both while growing up and while with that piece of shit pack.

My mate could shave her head and I would still find her the most beautiful woman in the world.

Devyn guided her to the salon chair and eased her in. And, yeah, his nostrils flared as he took in her scent. Sophie turned her head and looked into his face a moment before turning to look at me, her brow raised.

And her pupils were dilated.

Well, shit. Either she was attracted to this beta or she was nearing her heat cycle. Which meant I needed to get her home as soon as she was done before she sent me into rut. I would end up aggressive and possessive as fuck if she went into heat with a house full of alphas, whether they were bonded to Violet or not.

BY THE TIME Devyn had finished snipping and cutting her hair, Sophie looked like a whole different person.

No. She didn't *look* like a different person – it was obvious she *felt* like a different person as she held a mirror and turned her head this way and that.

The hair that had hung nearly to her waist was now a couple inches above her shoulders. There were layers and Devyn had used different tools to curl and style it. It was beautiful and framed her face perfectly but had a little sass to it instead of those perfectly smooth waves she'd worn to meet and then court packs.

Sassy hair to match my sassy mate.

"Do you like it?" she asked, her eyes finding me in the mirror as I stood behind her.

"It's perfect," I said.

Her smile stretched and nothing short of love filled her pretty brown eyes.

Setting the mirror down, she turned and lifted her face, waiting for me to press a kiss to her lips. We hadn't shared much physical intimacy since last night. I was giving her time. I would give her as much time as she needed. But the second she was ready, I had every intention of latching my teeth onto her shoulder and making her mine forever, with or without a fucking bonding ceremony.

"Give them a second," Chase said from behind us.

After pressing a soft kiss to Sophie's lips, I stepped back and turned to look over my shoulder.

"Chase likes to spend money on me. And I have way too much of… well, everything. So, we're going to go shopping in my closet."

"I can't go in your bedroom, Violet," Sophie said as Devyn removed the cape he had draped around her.

The puff of fabric wafted Sophie's sweet caramel and floral scent mixed with something else…something clean and fresh and appealing. Fuck. Devyn. Was Violet trying to play matchmaker since Sophie and I were officially a pack of two?

Ignoring the way my dick twitched at the scent combination, I followed the alphas through the house while Violet practically dragged Sophie upstairs and into her bedroom. I could hear them chatting and giggling. And my heart swelled at the sounds. It would take far longer than a day, far longer than a few weeks for Sophie to heal from what she'd endured.

And I would be there every step of the way to make sure she was glued back together. I would gladly tear pieces of myself away to patch her up.

Sophie

VIOLET HAD PILED clothes nearly as tall as me on her bed and ruffled through them piece by piece, holding them up to me and either dropping them in the *keep* or *no* pile.

"I can't take your clothes, Violet. Besides, your boobs are huge. Nothing will fit me."

"Not like I'm giving you bras," she teased. "Chase is always buying me crap. I have way more than I can wear. Oh! Do you have a nest at Kai's? Do you need anything?" She waved her hand in the air when I opened my mouth to argue. "I don't mean my personal stuff. There's a whole closet full of omega comfort crap the guys keep buying. I haven't used any of it so it doesn't smell like me. And, even if my pack's scents are on it, you can use scent blockers. At least for your first heat. Because, sister, you are close."

Yeah. I was. I'd been fighting it the whole time I was with Anton and the others, praying that I wouldn't have to suffer with them through what should have been a time of bonding.

Being with Kai last night, sleeping with him pressing me into the cushions of the couch, did something to my omega, reminded her she was safe, that I was safe. And the first tiny cramps had started low in my belly this morning.

Meeting Devyn hadn't helped. I wasn't quite ready to entertain adding anyone to what I was building with Kai. But...would having a beta as sweet as Devyn in our life be such a bad thing?

That was something we would discuss at a later time, like long after my heat, after my heart, mind, and body had healed, after we had begun to build a life together.

After my mate officially claimed me.

I needed his bite. I needed his mark. I needed to know no one would ever tear us apart again. Once I carried his mark, no one could do a damn thing about it.

I hadn't bothered calling my parents yet. I was sure Anton had already called my fathers and made up all kinds of lies. My phone was at their house. I hadn't bothered grabbing anything when Kai had carried me from the house. I didn't want a single thing back there.

Honestly, there was a part of me that didn't care whether I spoke to another family member again. They didn't love me. They didn't care about me. They cared about my designation and what that could mean for their own lives, their own status in society.

I'd meant what I'd said last night – fuck them. Fuck anyone who thought omegas were to be used and abused. Fuck anyone who thought my designation determined my future.

"I don't know if there's a nest at Kai's. I don't think he'd planned on ever having an omega," I admitted.

I would need something soon, though, at least some soft blankets when the pain and fever took over.

She waved her hand in the air and went back to digging through clothes. "We'll ask him when we go back downstairs. Oh! What about this one?" she asked as she held up a dress for my opinion before holding it against my body.

We weren't the same size, I was inches shorter than her, and she was very well endowed in the breast area. But...I literally had nothing to my name. I would need at least some shorts and tees until I could find a job to buy my own clothes.

"So..." Violet started, her eyes on the stack of keeps that she was folding nicely. "I was talking to Chase."

When she didn't say anything else, I sat on the edge of the bed and waited.

"And...did you know Chase is loaded? It's not something he brags about, but his parents and grandparents left him this crazy big inheritance. That's why he's always trying to buy me stuff. But...what if we were to become investors?"

When I didn't speak, she turned to look at me.

"In your organization. To help omegas."

"What?" I whispered as her words began to register in my mind.

"I'm an omega, too. I don't know if you know how I met my pack but...I was in a compound. Traffickers had stalked me and taken me.

They…they were there to free us. I was one of only a few who made it out alive. And we just happened to click and fall in love. There needs to be…something needs to change. And I believe you're the start to that change."

I had told Violet about my ideas and plans the night she and her pack had come to hang out at the halfway house what felt like years ago but had only been less than a couple of months.

"Really?" Hope and doubt warred within me.

"Someone has to start the change. And you're smart. And strong. And you have an amazing alpha who would turn the world upside down to help you. And…you now have a super cool best friend who happens to have a super loaded mate who adores me."

"I heard that," Chase said as he stood in the door.

"She's not lying," Liam said from behind him. "You girls hungry? Andrei and Mac are talking about grilling."

A small cramp fluttered low in my belly. My heat was coming. Which meant there would be time where I wouldn't be coherent enough to acknowledge my physical hunger or thirst. Might as well take advantage of the time while I had it.

"I could eat," I said.

"I'm starving," Violet said. "They're trying to knock me up, so we've been expending a lot of calories," she explained as though we were discussing the weather.

"Violet," Chase said with a surprised chuckle. "You're getting as bad as Liam."

CHAPTER 19

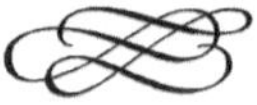

Kai

When Sophie descended the stairs with Violet, Liam, and Chase, she shook her head and smiled at me. Liam and Chase were carrying several bags of, I assumed, clothing.

"I need to talk to you," she whispered, taking my hand and dragging me from the room.

Her scent was still sweet, no bitterness to alert me to any fear. Instead, she looked elated. Excited.

"What's up?" I asked, opening my arms when she stepped forward and hugging her tightly to me.

I really did like her new haircut. It fit that fiery personality that had snared me – and irritated me – from the beginning.

"I was talking to Violet," she said, her smile widening into a grin. "Her pack wants to invest in Omega Change."

My brows pinched together in confusion as I continued to smile down at her.

"That's what I'm going to call it. My company. Omega Change. Like…mega change. Or major change?"

"Clever." And then her words sank in. "Wait…they're going to invest. They're going to help you get it started?"

"Yep," she said, her grin wide, all teeth and full lips.

"Holy shit, princess," I said, hugging her tightly and lifting her from the ground.

She giggled against my throat, pressing her lips there and burying her nose, inhaling my scent deeply.

When I set her back down, I couldn't release my hold on her, not yet. I'd only gotten her back in my life last night. Not even twenty-four hours. It would take far longer before I would be content letting her out of my sight without worrying someone would hurt her again, that someone would take her away from me again.

"Are you still okay with it? With me working? With me spending long hours doing research, interviewing people to help, spending long hours in an office?"

"Why would I have a problem with that? Especially since I plan to spend those hours with you in the office as much as possible."

Her smile faltered and doubt entered her eyes. "Why?"

"Why what?"

"Why would you be at the office, too?"

"The omegas who come to you will need security as much as you. I'm going to help build a network of security for both private and public protection."

"What about your job with ORE?"

I shrugged up a shoulder. "I'm still displaced without a team. I'll keep my job there and still accept positions. Not living with another omega, of course. But…between missions, I'll help you build a security network while you work on the stuff that requires that big brain of yours."

She nearly melted into my arms, nuzzling her cheek against my chest. "Life is going to be…different," she said softly. "We won't be, I don't know…we won't be a normal pair."

"Do you like Devyn?" I asked, and instantly wished I could have shoved my foot into my mouth.

She lifted her head and narrowed her eyes at me. "Why do you ask?"

"He's nice. And you looked like you appreciated his scent. He's a beta so I won't feel the need to beat the shit out of him for being near you. And...he could join us, join our pack."

"Wait...do *you* like him?" she asked as her smile grew into a knowing grin.

I wasn't quite ready to admit his scent had made my dick twitch, especially when it had swirled and mixed with my beautiful omega's.

WE HAD BARELY MADE it through dinner. As the minutes ticked on to hours, tightness had entered her face and I'd caught her placing a shaky hand to her lower abdomen more than once. When I would touch her or brush against her, her skin was hot. My sweet omega was going into heat.

Thank fuck it would happen with me and not back at that fucking house with those fucking assholes who I still had the urge to kill. Every glimpse of the bruises they'd left on her soft skin sent a fresh wave of rage coursing through me, but I had to push it away and focus on Sophie's needs.

She shifted constantly in the passenger seat, clenching her thighs together, whimpering as wave after wave of pain began to wash over her.

"We're almost home, princess."

I didn't have a nest. I had the one bedroom. Even the sole closet in my bedroom wasn't big enough to fill with blankets and pillows for her. We would have to make do, pile as much soft shit on the bed as possible to make her comfortable.

She stumbled from the passenger seat as I opened the door and tried to help her to the porch. She was practically leaning against me as I wrapped an arm around her shoulders and guided her into my house.

I needed to make so many changes to the place to make it perfect for my omega. Perfect for my mate. Perfect for Sophie.

But right now, I needed to get as many bottles of water and some easy to grab food in the bedroom before she was lost to her heart and would forget simple things like eating and drinking.

"You're burning up," I said as I guided her to the bedroom.

"Hurts," she whimpered. That sound broke my heart and awakened the alpha inside of me. I had to take care of my omega, needed to ease her discomfort.

"Do you want a bath? It'll help bring down the fever."

"You. I need you," she begged, her hands tight in my t-shirt even as she practically collapsed onto the bed, dragging me with her.

"I'm here, sweetheart. I'll never leave you again. I swear to you. I swear on everything I am I will never leave your side again."

How the hell had she avoided going into heat with the other alphas? I'd heard through the years that an omega could often skip her heat if she didn't feel safe, if she didn't feel cherished. I'd also heard that an omega's heat could be brought on quicker in the presence of her true alpha. And that was me. I knew that months ago as much as I knew that now.

She was mine. And I belonged to her – heart, mind, body, and soul. She could have any part of me. I was lost to this woman, addicted to her scent, to her voice.

Her pupils were blown until there was barely the tiniest hint of brown. Her face was flushed and sweat gave her face a dewy look. Her lips were parted, her breathing was shallow. She was going into heat fast and hard.

Without waiting, I removed my shirt first, then began to strip her of the clothes she'd borrowed from Violet before we'd visited Omega Rescue and Extraction headquarters. I wasn't sure if Violet wanted them back, so I was careful not to pop the buttons or rip the fabric, although all I wanted to do was tear the material to shreds to so I could get to her faster.

Sophie had been through so much in the short time we'd been apart. I wished we could have had time to reconnect before her body and her hormones took over, before she struggled to form a coherent thought.

"Tell me how I can help," I said as I gently dragged her pants over her legs then laid her back on the bed.

"My skin is so hot," she whined, the sound breaking my heart. "It hurts. Everything hurts."

For the briefest of moments, a fleeting thought passed through my mind, a wish that we'd met Devyn in enough time before Sophie's heat. I had thought I'd lost her. I could easily go into rut and the last thing I would ever do was hurt her. If the beta was here, he would help keep us both calm, could keep his head on straight to make sure we took breaks to rest and eat.

But he wasn't. Not this time.

I had never wanted a pack. I had never wanted an omega. Now I wanted to give Sophie the world, and that happened to include adding members to our family that could not only protect her from the outside world but from her own fucking alpha.

Sophie

KAI'S FINGERS were gentle as he caressed my face, dragging a cool cloth across my forehead, dabbing at the sweat dampening my chest.

I didn't want the washcloth. I didn't want gentle caresses. I wanted the pain to go away, and there was only way for that to happen.

"Please, Kai," I begged, shifting my legs and rubbing my thighs together in hopes of adding enough friction to ease the pressure building.

"I'm here, princess."

Princess. The word he'd used as a taunt in the beginning now sounded like the sweetest praise coming from his lips.

Dropping the cloth onto the floor, he pushed from the side of the bed and fumbled with the button and zipper of his jeans. I rolled onto my side and cupped his hard length through his pants, whimpering when his hips pushed forward, and he hissed in a breath.

"Patience, sweetheart," he said with a strained chuckle.

Through my lust hazed brain, I looked into his face, into his beautiful crystalline blue eyes. Veins bulged on his throat as though he was straining to keep from pouncing on me and slamming his cock into my slick coated pussy. Which was exactly what I wanted, what my body needed.

Was he afraid he would hurt me? Did he worry he would scare me?

Or was he holding onto a thread to avoid going into rut?

Rut sounded good to me right about now as another cramp squeezed my ovaries and made me cry out. I could have sworn Kai could have fried an egg on my forehead at this point.

I was so thankful I was with my love, with my mate, with my true alpha during this. I couldn't image the joy my pain would have brought Anton, how he might have treated me when I was fully out of my mind as my hormones took over and my hindbrain was in full control.

Kai's cock jutted forth the moment he shoved his pants down his legs, the precum at his slit causing my core to ache and my mouth to water.

Before he could stop me, I lunged forward and lapped at that moisture, humming with approval at the sweet warm flavor. More. I needed more.

Wrapping my lips around his girth, I took him as deep as I could until my nose bumped his knot.

"Fuck," Kai grunted, gripping my hair tightly and gently pulling me away. "I'll let you taste me later, princess. Let's get your pain and fever under control first."

And then he was climbing onto the bed, forcing me backward as he hovered over me, our lips inches apart as we shared breath. His lips were soft yet hungry as he kissed me, fucking my mouth with his tongue as he pushed my thighs apart with his knees and settled between them.

The head of his cock brushed along my slicked and needy cunt, and I moaned into his mouth. He swallowed the sound then pushed forward, feeding me inch by agonizing inch of the cock I'd feared I would never feel again.

There was something about Kai, had been something about Kai that made me feel whole, like he was my home. It felt as though our bodies had been made specifically for each other, fitting as perfectly as a key and lock.

"Fuuuck," he ground out, burying his face in my neck as he nipped and sucked on my shoulder, my neck, craning his neck to try to press kisses to my chest. He was too tall. Or I was too short.

I wanted his lips on my breasts, wrapped around my nipples. But this angle wouldn't allow that. And I sure as hell couldn't handle it if he pulled from me. His cock inside of me was already erasing some of the cramping, easing some of the pain.

More.

In a slow rhythm, he began to pump into me, rotating his hips until his swollen, throbbing knot was rubbing and bumping against my clit, pushing the pressure high, higher, and then I was falling as explosions went off behind my closed lids and I cried out his name.

"That's right, princess. I want you to feel good."

He kept fucking into me, his thrusts growing more frantic, needier, more desperate. And that pressure began to build again. One orgasm wouldn't be nearly enough to ease the symptoms of my cycle. This was merely the start of a week full of our bodies being connected, of him filling me over and over with his cock, his fingers, his tongue...

His knot.

One hand smoothed over my hair as he lifted his head to stare into my face. "So fucking beautiful," he murmured, nothing short of reverence in his husky tone.

That hand trailed lower until he cupped my breast, rolling a pebbled nipple between his forefinger and thumb.

And then his fingers slid down between where our bodies met and he teased my clit as my body began to clench, my core fluttering around him.

"Mmmm. I can feel your wet pussy clenching my dick. You ready for another one, princess?"

"Yes. Please. Fuck. Yes. Knot. Please, Kai. I need your knot."

"One more, princess. I want to feel your greedy little pussy clamp around me one more time and I'll give you my knot."

As he fondled and pinched my clit, that same pressure built and built and then my body tensed, my mouth opening on a silent scream as I fell apart, my pussy doing exactly as he'd asked and clenching around him.

"That's my beautiful girl."

Grabbing my thighs gently, he steadied me then pushed forward until my opening stretched and his knot bedded inside of me, rubbing every inch of my inner walls until a surprise orgasm tore through me.

My hands shot out and gripped his forearms, my nails biting into his skin as I scrambled for words, as my mouth opened and a scream rent from my chest.

His weight dropped onto me, barely held up on his forearms, and he rutted inside of me, grunts filling the air until hot jets filled me, his dick twitching over and over until our release and my slick began to seep out and run down the crack of my ass.

The pain had subsided. The fever had lowered.

And then, within minutes, the need rose again like a tidal wave and I was clawing at Kai, begging him to move, begging him to touch me, begging him to knot me again.

I was in heat. But I was madly in love with this man. I was addicted to my own personal drug. And I knew I would never tire of feeling the way he stretched me, the way he looked into my eyes as though I was the most precious thing in the world.

CHAPTER 20

Kai

Sophie was cradled in my lap as we struggled to stay awake through a movie. Her heat had lasted five days. My dick was sore. My sac was empty. And I loved every fucking second of it.

I'd feared that once her hindbrain was no longer in charge, she would start to retreat into herself, that the damage done by Anton would sneak back into her mind and the shame would return.

The bruises were there, would be there for at least another week, but she was a fighter. I'd caught her staring off into space as though returning to that pack house, but I'd guided her back to the present with soft kisses to the mark I'd left on her shoulder. She was mine. Forever.

Even now, I could feel her emotions deep in my chest. She was tired, exhausted, but she was happy. But under that happiness, that peace, was underlying stress and anxiety.

She had yet to contact her family. She'd left her phone behind with the rest of her belongings so there had been no barrage of phone calls.

But she would eventually have to call them, tell them she'd left the pack, tell them she'd found her true alpha.

Tell them she was bonded and would no longer follow their rules.

And I would be by her side the entire time. If her fathers – or anyone else – thought they would try to drag her away, they would have to go through me. And I had a feeling Violet's pack would fight just as fiercely to protect her. Not only was it their job as members of ORE, but they loved Violet and she and Sophie had become fast friends.

"Violet gave me a lot of clothes, but I don't know how much of it will fit," she muttered then yawned.

"We'll go shopping. Get you some business suits so you'll look all professional when you open Omega Change."

She made a dismissive sound in the back of her throat, but I could feel the burst of joy through our bond. She was excited to get started. And I was excited to do everything I could to make her dream happen.

"Do you think they'll get in trouble?" she asked after a few minutes of silence.

"I don't know," I answered honestly. I knew exactly who she was thinking of without her voicing their names.

I wanted to tell her absolutely yes, Anton, at least, would do some time for abusing an omega. For abusing a woman. A human. But he had money and power. And rich fuckers tended to skirt the edges of the judicial system more often than not.

"But I'll do everything I can to put pressure on my department."

She nestled against me again, her body beginning to relax. And then another little thrum of excitement and curiosity tickled over our bond.

"Can I ask you something else?"

Kissing her on the top of her head, I said, "You can ask me anything, princess."

"Devyn–"

I threw my head back and guffawed. "I knew you wanted him."

She rolled onto her back to look me in the face and the sweetest pink hue washed over her cheeks. "I know you don't want a full pack. It's just…"

She had asked for him during her heat. But I'd been nearly lost to my rut and hadn't wanted to take even the seconds it would have taken to call him in to help. He might have helped us, made sure we drank more water, made sure we rested more.

"I don't know what it is about him, but he makes me feel…kind of like you do."

A surge of jealousy coursed through me, and she shoved lightly at my chest when she felt that thread get plucked.

"I don't mean like that. I'm not in love with him. I just met him. I'm just saying, I don't know. I feel comfortable around him. He doesn't make me nervous. And he smells–"

"Fucking amazing," I finished for her.

She wiggled against me when she felt my cock start to harden again.

"Glad you agree."

Leaning forward, she nipped at my lips then nuzzled her nose against my neck. "No one will ever smell as delicious as you, though."

"You want to court him?"

She awkwardly shrugged up the shoulder that wasn't pinned against the couch. "We can talk about it. There is a whole lot to do before we can contemplate adding to our…family."

And that was exactly what the two of us were – a family.

"I eventually need to call my parents. I already know how that conversation will go, but…time to rip off the band-aid."

"Do you know their numbers by heart? You can use my phone."

She groaned and dropped a hand over her face. "Maybe courting the beta first is a good idea."

I chuckled and kissed her chin. "No reason to bring someone new in when we already have our hands full."

A beta would be calming to her. They soothed both omegas and alphas. But it wouldn't be fair to Devyn to bring him in right when we were dealing with legal battles, a fight with her family, and the beginning stages of opening something as important as Omega Change.

With a huff, she pushed up to sit and I groaned when the movement rubbed against my growing erection. Between having my sweet omega so close and then talking about the sexy ass beta, I was ready to go through another round of a week of being buried in her soaked cunt.

"What time is it?" she asked, looking around my tiny cabin.

She'd taken the short tour of the one bedroom, one bathroom, small kitchen/dining room combo, and the living room. And I hadn't felt an ounce of disgust or doubt in our bond. In fact, a sense of rightness had settled between us when she was done, as though she felt as though this was meant to be her home all along.

Unless, of course, she was serious about bringing someone into our tiny pack. I had never wanted a pack. I had never wanted an omega, either. But now that I had one, I wouldn't deny her anything. Even if that meant bringing in a whole gaggle of betas to keep her safe, to keep her company, and to give her pleasure.

But betas only. I knew myself too well. No fucking way would I share her with another alpha.

"Just after seven."

"I was hoping you'd say later. Then I could put off the call until tomorrow."

I looped an arm around her waist and kissed her shoulder. "You can put it off as long as you want."

Her short hair swayed as she shook her head. "Nope. I want to get this over with. Tell them where they can stick all those plans they made for me, deal with the Anton shit, then get Devyn over here so we can see if he tastes as good as he smells."

"Fuck, princess," I said, instantly reaching down to adjust my boner. "I think you need to stay away from Liam. He's rubbing off on you."

"Nah. This has always been me. I was just never allowed to show my flirty side, my playful side."

I'd seen those sides of her, and it occurred to me I might very well have been the first person in her life to have had that honor.

Sophie

I PACED the living room with Kai's phone clutched in my hand, staring at the screen and willing myself to bring it to life and dial the numbers.

Whoever I called would have Kai's number. I could make the call anonymous, but they would eventually discover I was bonded. And they would learn I was bonded to the man they'd hired to guard me while they sent prospective packs to court me.

Daddy Michael was the least reprehensive of the four alphas. Dialing his number, I took a deep breath, hit call, and brought the phone to my ear.

"Hello?" his deep voice answered.

"It's Sophia." Not Sophie. Never Sophie with my family.

I heard voices in the background and then they faded. A door closed and then Daddy Michael spoke. "What in the hell is going on? What happened? Your pack called. Said a group of alphas assaulted them and dragged you away."

"Lies."

"Excuse me?"

"Did you know anything about the pack Daddy Jim arranged me to meet? Any of the packs?"

Michael cleared his throat. "Jim and Johnathan handled that. I only knew their names and professions."

"I was courting a pack. I was living with them. They wanted to bond me."

"That's what Jim was told."

"And they abused me."

A soft gasp sounded over the phone the same time a rush of rage surged through my bond with Kai.

Turning my back to him, as though that would ease the rush of emotions, I focused on the conversation. "The pack leader said he was going to mold me into the perfect little omega. Like mom. He abused me, Michael." I couldn't even call him dad at this point. My own rage was mixing with Kai's now. "He threatened to dark bond me to control me. We had a dinner party. I invited a fellow omega and her alphas over."

"The guard who stayed with you…"

"Yep. He joined them. We fell in love while we were in that house together, Dad. I love him. More than I knew was possible." A surge of affection filled my heart. "But he was willing to let me go because the pack…they were full of shit and put on a good show. Like Jim and Johnathan do in public. But I'm not Mom. When Kai and my friends realized what was going on, they gave me the option. And I left willingly. I'm bonded now. Nothing you or the others say will change that."

A heavy sigh sounded like static over the line. I could almost picture Daddy Michael dropping into his leather chair at his desk. "Anton is threatening lawsuits. He's claiming that alpha stole his omega. And he's threatening to file assault charges."

"Let him. I already filed my own against him. And the alphas…they were all Omega Rescue and Extraction officers. They witnessed the whole thing. He can threaten whatever he wants. But if I have my way, he'll never have another omega in his life. I'm starting my organization like I always said I would. I have an investor. And my mate is handling the security side. So…I guess this is goodbye."

"Wait, why goodbye?"

I blinked a few times. Michael had never been as demanding and domineering as my other three fathers, but he'd never exactly been what anyone would consider loving or affectionate, either. I assumed he would be pissed that his remaining unbonded omega daughter wouldn't bring him and the family more prestige. I assumed he would be enraged that I'd bonded for love instead of power and money.

"I'm not returning to that life, Dad. I'm doing exactly what I always planned. I have an alpha who loves me. And…we might even build a pack together." I looked over my shoulder and winked at Kai, pulling a smile from him.

He sighed again. "This isn't goodbye. I get you don't want anything to do with the others, but you know I'm here if you need anything. Within reason."

"Within reason," I repeated. Because, even if he did love me in his own way, there were things he wouldn't do like sully his pack's name or reputation.

"Talk later?" he asked, an odd lilt of hope in his voice.

"Yeah. Talk later."

I ended the call. No one in my family ever said I love you before they hung up or parted ways. They never said those three words for any reason. I'd heard them for the first time in my entire life when they'd left Kai's lips.

I set Kai's phone on the coffee table and turned to face him. "That…was easier than I thought it would be."

"Already announcing to the world that we're thinking about growing our pack?" he teased.

But there was the slightest hint of anxiety in our bond. He was worried about me.

"I should have told him I was going to add a bunch of omegas to our pack. That would have really freaked him out."

Kai grunted as I practically launched myself onto him. "Right. Because you'd be willing to share your alpha with another omega."

"You're willing to share your omega with a beta," I said.

He raised one brow. "First of all, I said we would talk about possibly courting Devyn. Second…let me paint you a picture."

He described, in detail, exactly what would happen if there was more than one omega in the house, how I would have to wait my turn for his attention, how I wouldn't be the only one being spoiled.

"You're right. I could never have a house full of omegas."

Kai

I HAD ALREADY KNOWN I wouldn't be able to deny Sophie anything. And I'd meant it when I told her that we should probably hold off on courting Devyn until our lives had calmed down.

But she wanted the beta. In the short time they'd been together while he'd done her hair, something had formed between them, a sort of bond. And I assumed it was primarily biological. Or at least that was how it had started.

Sophie had waited all of two weeks before broaching the subject again. And Devyn had been over the moon with the prospect of spending time with us. Not just Sophie, but the two of us. Apparently, my scent had appealed to him as strongly as his had to me.

I had never pictured myself as the kind of man who would willingly share the love of my life with anyone. But sitting on the couch, watching as Sophie straddled Devyn's lap, nipping and tasting his lips, while I rested my hands on her hips and urged her up and down on his cock, I found myself feeling an odd sense of fullness.

I'd already tasted the beta's lips many times and had found myself almost as drunk as I had the first time I had kissed my omega.

In the short time we'd spent with Devyn, he was quickly becoming family. While he didn't mind being a bottom for me, he sure as fuck loved taking our omega hard and fast. And the man's mouth was fucking magical.

Eventually, we'd asked him to move into the house with us, the three of us sharing my king-sized bed. We were already making plans of finding something bigger so we could all have a little more space.

And in hopes of adding maybe another member to the pack in the future. And at least one child.

CHAPTER 21

Sophie

"We can provide housing and security for as long as you need," I told the omega across from me. "We also offer scholarships or technical training if you're interested in furthering your education or entering the workforce."

"What about when I'm at work, though?" the young woman asked, fear entering her wide eyes.

I held up a hand to calm her. "We provide references for either fully beta owned and run or secured professions. At no point would you be at risk while working. We can also provide security to and from your job until you've found a pack. *If* that's something you're interested in."

"I mean, yeah. Someday. I just presented, though." And she was barely eighteen. She had plenty of time to worry about things like packs and mating. She would, however, require assistance through her cycles.

"Now we get to talk about the embarrassing stuff," I said, leaning forward on my forearms. "Do you have someone you trust to help you through your cycles, or will you need assistance?"

Another part of the organization I'd made sure to implement as soon as possible were heat helpers as well as stocking up on...silicone items such as knots that would help. Kai and his friends had scoured applications and made sure each alpha was trustworthy and well trained in how to care for a needy omega. They'd been through dozens of medical tests and would continue to be tested between each assignment.

"I need–" Her voice squeaked out at first. She cleared her throat then tried again. "I don't have any one to help."

I made notes in the omega's file that would be locked securely in the file cabinet in my office. And the entire building not only had top of the line security systems complete with cameras but was guarded overnight due to the temporary apartments that held displaced omegas.

"We'll make sure you'll have everything you need. Here," I said, handing her my card. "Keep this on you at all times. I'll have one of the guards show you to your apartment and then we'll get everything lined up over the next few weeks. If you're heat comes sooner than you expect, let either one of the guards or me know and we'll make sure you're safe and comfortable."

The smile the omega gave me filled me with the same sense of joy and pride that I had every time I knew I'd helped someone's life become that much easier.

She stood and I nodded to one of the men Kai had hired. This was a beta, but big enough and intimidating enough to be every bit an alpha. But, like Kai, he was a big ol' teddy bear and always softened when in the presence of an omega.

"Could you show Mae to her apartment? And make sure the pantry and fridge are stocked. Let Joy know if it's lacking anything."

Joy was my newest hire. She was supposed to be my personal

assistant but had ended up being a damn life saver. She had a hand in nearly everything and helped me run this company smoothly.

The door opened and I smiled as warmth spread through my bond before I even lifted my head to see my mate strolling through the door – Devyn right beside him.

We'd been courting the beta, but it had been strained. Not because of Devyn; the beta was nearly perfect. But…

"You're working way too many hours," Kai said as he bent to press a kiss to my lips then bent to press one to my swollen belly.

"Hey, you agreed you wouldn't have a problem with it. Not my fault you knocked me up."

"*Oh, alpha. I need your knot,*" he mimicked, even raising his voice an octave to impersonate me. At least he'd kept his voice low.

I giggled and swatted at him as he nuzzled my shoulder, pressing wet kisses over his claiming mark.

"You need to slow down before you end up giving birth in this damn office," he said with an affectionate smile.

I waved him off and set Mae's folder aside. "I've got at least another month. Joy has been handling the bulk of everything, anyway. Hey, honey," I greeted Devyn as he leaned down to press a soft kiss to my lips. "What have you boys been up to today?"

The blush on Devyn's cheeks and the hint of lust through the bond told me I'd missed a lot of fun while I'd been hard at work.

"You couldn't at least wait until I got home. You know how horny pregnancy hormones make me."

Both men barked out a laugh. I'd been horny since the day Kai and I had been reunited. It had only amplified when we'd invited Devyn to start spending time with us.

At least I knew it was Kai's pup I was carrying. Since we were only courting Devyn, we'd all agreed to a few ground rules, and Kai's biggest one was that he was the only one allowed to fuck my pussy during my heat.

And Devyn sure as hell didn't seem to mind, using his mouth and fingers to help when Kai needed a short break.

"How much longer do you have? We're starving," Devyn asked.

"I was actually almost done. Uh…" I craned my neck. "Will you see if you can hunt down Wilder, Keaton, and Oksana?"

Kai's brows drew together. "Why?"

"I have an assignment for the three of them. An omega who has no one to watch over him while he interviews prospective packs." Like deva vu. I was assigning guards to watch over him while he went through the same process I had over a year ago.

At least this omega was choosing his own path. He wanted a pack and had agreed to allow us to vet the packs first. That way, we would know he was safe regardless.

"You're putting Oksana and Keaton together?" Kai laughed darkly. "Oh, Wilder is going to have a blast with that one," he said as he turned and went in search of the three in question.

"Do I want to know?" Devyn asked.

"Old rivalry. If Lily had a dick, I would say they were comparing dick sizes every time they were around each other. They're always trying to out alpha the other one."

Devyn shook his head and lowered into a chair.

We had done the exact opposite of what we'd agreed and invited him into our lives before we knew what would happen with Anton. And, in the end, the asshole had gotten off with nothing more than a slap on the wrist, just as Kai had warned.

But I was in a position of power myself, now. While I couldn't protect every omega on the planet, I would do everything in my control to make sure that asshole never had the privilege of so much as breathing the same air of another omega again.

I could hear the voices rising from the other side of the building and bit back a smile. I'd intentionally thrown Wilder in there for two reasons – Violet trusted him, so I trusted him. And he was a beta. My hopes were that he would be a cool head if the two alphas got riled up in the presence of the rare male omega.

And if the four of them fell in love….

Kai

. . .

"SHE'S SO BEAUTIFUL," I said for probably the hundredth time as I stared down at the sleeping bundle in my arms.

Sophie hadn't gotten her wish of working for another month. She'd gone into labor two weeks later. Not technically early, but it had still made me nervous that it was before the official due date.

Now, she rested on the hospital bed, smiling wistfully at me as I held our first child. Our daughter. She had my blue eyes and Sophie's honey blonde hair. She was perfect and tiny and felt so fragile in my big hands.

"You can let her rest in the bassinet," Sophie said, a smile in her voice.

"I'm not done staring at her yet."

"Did you want to count her fingers and toes again?"

I smiled at my mate. I couldn't get enough of that beautiful face as she beamed at me with so much love and pride. And I couldn't believe I was holding my child in my arms, my daughter. I was mated. I was a father. And Devyn was pack, even if we hadn't made it official.

He'd been as over the moon as I was when Sophie had declared her water had broken. He'd paced outside the hospital room until I told him he could come in just time to see little Lara Elizabeth Lanse enter the world.

I had let our beta hold her for a few minutes then demanded her back. He could try to knock Sophie up another time. But this was my turn. This was my child. My family.

"Where's Devyn?" Sophie asked.

"He headed down to the cafeteria. Said the food they brought was nasty and you needed something more filling."

For a beta, he sure as hell was having fun spoiling our omega. Especially since she'd gotten pregnant. He would spend hours rubbing her sore feet, waited on her hand and foot. I had started to grow jealous until I realized he was doting on me as much as her. He was making it so I wouldn't have to leave my omega's side any longer than necessary.

Which was what convinced me he was definitely meant to be with us.

"She'll need a brother," I said more to myself than anyone else. "Someone to watch over her and scare the boys away."

"How about we focus on getting through the next few months of no sleep before we talk about more babies?" she said around a wide yawn.

"Go to sleep. I've got this."

"Are you going to sit there and stare at her for the next few hours?"

I bent and pressed a kiss to Sophie's forehead. "Not the whole time. I'll be staring at you, too. I love you, princess. I'll love you forever."

Her eyes fluttered closed a second before she whispered, "I'll love you forever," back.

* * *

If you loved Sophie story of discovering her inner strength, finding her love, and building a family, I would love if you could take the time to leave a review on your favorite site.

You can contact Raelynn Rose at authorraelynnrose@yahoo.com

Wait! Have you joined the party yet? Oops…I meant the newsletter! Keep up to date on releases, cover reveals, and giveaway, as well as a novella of the story of Kai, Sophie, and Devyn. You can join here!

9 781949 447903